DUELING THE DEVIL

A SPECULATIVE FICTION NOVELLA

THE NEXT HIGH PRIEST SERIES
BOOK 3

PETER DEHAAN

- Copyeditor: Robyn Mulder
- Cover design: Fanderclai Design
- Author photo: Chelsie Jensen Photography

To all who stand against tyranny.

CONTENTS

DUELING THE DEVIL

In a world just like ours . . . only different

In his lust for power, the sorry man yielded to temptation and gave his soul to the devil. —History 12.17

1

WHO'S IN CHARGE?

Emma had never liked Pompous Jack, and she certainly didn't trust him. But until now she had no reason to fear him. She locked eyes with the evil man. "That sounded like a threat."

"Oh, you so amuse me, little one. I never make threats, just promises." He stared down at her. The corners of his lips twitched up ever so slightly. "You can make this easy or you can make it hard."

"So can you!" Emma brought her hand to her hip and glared, just like she'd seen her mom do when she wanted to make a point.

"You're but an insignificant child. I won't tolerate you telling a man of my stature what to do. Remember my standing as His Royal Eminence."

Junior stood next to Emma, but at a respectful half a step back. He served as the priest assigned to her, but this wasn't his fight. This contest was her versus Pompous Jack. She had no doubt.

What she wasn't sure about was if their confrontation was limited to the physical realm or if it would extend into the spiritual one too. According to Gabe, her trusted mentor, Pompous Jack's glossy black appearance in the spiritual realm confirmed he'd given himself over to the devil, whose presence filled his soul. This made him a most dangerous man, perhaps almost as dangerous as the devil himself.

"I'm also the High Priestess." Emma squared herself to him and narrowed her gaze. "According to the Holy Text, I'm in charge. You're not. So back down."

"Do you really think I care what that outdated tome says? Despite some antiquated book, I am, in fact, in charge. Once I prove you're a fraud, you'll be out of here so fast it will make your head spin."

Emma thrust her index finger at his gaunt face. "I can say the same about you." With the Sovereign on her side, she had nothing to fear. Still, concern taunted her for the first time since she had become the new High Priestess, a role she didn't want and wasn't ready for. Yet the Sovereign had picked her —a mere teenager—to lead the people.

With their eyes still locked, Pompous Jack spoke first, but without yielding in their contest of wills. "Are you going to stand here all night and stare at me?"

Normally, she'd be up for the challenge. Last time she bested him, but not tonight. Though she didn't want to blink first, the threats she'd endured at school all day left her emotionally drained. Persisting in a staring contest was the last thing she wanted to do. Exhaustion plagued her, and she looked away. Even more, she needed to recharge her soul. She would deal with him tomorrow.

"Go to your room!" He pointed a bony finger at the Temple Palace. "And if you know what's good for you, you'll stay out of my way."

"I'll only obey the Sovereign. I don't care what you say." Emma stomped off.

"Don't you dare walk away from me, you ungrateful brat."

Emma spun around and raised her chin. "Don't tell me what to do! I turn you over to the Sovereign for the punishment you deserve."

Pompous Jack's lanky frame sagged.

Emma left him standing in a daze at the palace

entry. She marched toward the front door, with Junior striding to catch up. He reached the door first and opened it for her. She accepted his gesture with appreciation as he guided her to her quarters.

With head held high, she strode into the High Priest's residence in the palace, pulled the door shut, and clicked the lock. She exhaled slowly, slid to the floor, and cradled her head in her arms.

Oh, Sovereign, give me strength to stand against that evil man.

2

FIRST THINGS FIRST

With no homework to do—the only good thing that had happened all day—Emma moved directly into her routine of studying the Holy Text. She placed it on the floor like usual, with her notebook next to it. She lit the two candles and turned out the lights. After completing her ritual of seeking the Sovereign's insight, she read the next passage.

But she had trouble focusing.

The ordeals she had suffered in school that day preoccupied her. The threats. The tension. The reality that no one wanted her there. She would not go back. She'd take Captain Hernandez's advice and investigate homeschooling or distance learning.

What about Chloe, her BFF? What about her new boyfriend, Joshua? Was their relationship over even though it had barely begun?

Yet as soon as she shoved these concerns aside, in flooded worries about all the problems at the Temple grounds.

First was the overworked and underpaid staff, which implied problems with finances. Where was all the money going? She'd have to dig into that. Maybe her CPA mom could help. Next were the lazy priests who did little and expected much. She also dreamed of restarting the Temple school to train future priests, both male and female. She also wanted to help her new friends here: Topher and Ashley's barred relationship. Topher's bedridden dad. Jennifer's desire to teach. Then there was long-suffering Junior, whom Pompous Jack treated so poorly.

After two hours, she still stared at the same passage and hadn't made a single note in her journal. She hoped the Sovereign would forgive her lack of focus. She blew out the candles and went to bed.

The first time she had met success in seeking the Sovereign, her spirit had left her body and ascended into heaven. There she talked with the Almighty in the spiritual realm, begging for a new High Priest to restore balance in an out-of-balance world. She never dreamed she would assume that role—nor did she want it—but that's exactly what the Sovereign did.

Recalling that ethereal experience, she willed her spirit to separate from her body again and ascend. It didn't. She prayed for it to happen and tried anew. Straining every bit of her being, her spirit separated from her body and began a slow upward trek. Yet it stopped a mere three feet into its journey and slammed back into her body. Violently.

Distraught, she gazed into the spiritual realm, just as Gabe had taught her. She saw only black around her. An evil foreboding assaulted her. Aside from the bright white light emanating from her spirit, darkness surrounded her. As she peered into it, she made out dark forms flying around her, weaving in and out of each other in chaotic mayhem. Their eerie murmurings grew louder. The devil was at work and his evil minions were barring her from visiting the Sovereign in heaven.

She prayed aloud, so that the demons could hear. They recoiled at her bold declarations of faith. The white aura surrounding her grew, pushing back their evil. She recited Scripture from the Holy Text and sang her favorite songs of worship. Her bubble of safety grew, providing a protective hedge around her. Yet each time she paused, evil reclaimed the space they had ceded.

What am I doing wrong? Can I only access heaven from inside the ancient Temple?

Giving up any hope of direct interaction with the Sovereign tonight, she asked for direction. "Sovereign Lord, show me what to do. May your Divine Spirit guide me in what I need to do here to make things better and to honor you."

The Sovereign had spoken to her in the past, implanting words of supernatural instruction in her. Each time the Almighty had told her precisely what to do at that moment, but no more. Yet each act of obedience prepared her to receive the next instruction. Could the Sovereign's unspoken direction penetrate the oppressive dome of evil that surrounded her?

Of course it can, came the Sovereign's immediate response.

Tension eased from Emma's body, replaced with a supernatural peace. *What should I do?* Emma asked. *I'm so overwhelmed.*

First things first. Start with the priests. Divide them into three groups.

How? Why? Then what?

I'll tell you when the time comes. Trust me.

Emma believed the Sovereign would do just that. Relieved, she fell asleep, dreaming of what the future might bring.

3

A NEW DAY DAWNS

"**B**reakfast is served, Emma," Jennifer called with a welcome tap on her bedroom door.

Rejuvenated by a good night's rest, Emma had already pushed the turmoil of yesterday behind her. Today was a new day. She'd asked the Sovereign to guide her in making the most of the opportunity the day provided. She was ready, more than ready.

Joyed to see her new friend, Emma followed Jennifer to the palace dining room. They sat next to each other. Emma offered a prayer of blessing for their food. Having just begun to eat, Pompous Jack paraded into the space and interrupted their bliss.

His intense glare shifted from Emma to Jennifer. Her frame tensed.

"Assume your proper place, insubordinate!"

Jennifer leapt to her feet, almost tipping the chair over in her haste. She retreated to the wall and pressed against it. Shoulders back, she stared straight ahead. With elbows jutting out to her sides, she interlocked her fingers in front of her in the prescribed stance. "Forgive me, Your Royal Eminence."

"I'll deal with your defiance later. As you await the consequences, contemplate the reason why you're here . . . and if you deserve to remain a Temple employee."

Emma opened her mouth to protest, but he held up a hand to stop her. His head pivoted her way.

"I'm sure you now realize that you can't continue going to school as you had in the past. Your presence there serves as an interruption, and they can't ensure your safety. I can."

Though Emma agreed with the first part of what he said, his tone for the second part concerned her. "I've already decided I'm not going back. I want to look at homeschooling instead."

"There is no need. I've already decided how to proceed. I've arranged for Principal Johnson to send a tutor to work with you so you can complete your requisite education in safety here at the Temple Palace."

"Can Jennifer tutor me instead?"

"Don't make me laugh, my naïve little one. Do you really expect a simpleminded food server to function as your teacher?"

"She has her degree and is certified. So, yes, I do expect that."

"That's out of the question, especially given today's shenanigans." He glanced at his watch. "Your real tutor will be here in twenty-eight minutes. She'll meet with you in your study. Don't be late."

Emma waited for him to leave and then turned to Jennifer. "I'm so sorry about how he treated you. Don't worry, I'll take care of it."

"Don't give it another thought . . . My Lord." Jennifer continued staring straight ahead. Her eyelids fluttered. "I clearly overstepped my position and deserve whatever punishment I receive."

Emma stood and approached her friend, reaching out to hold her hand, but Jennifer remained frozen until she said, "May I remind you, My Lord, that your tutoring begins in twenty-seven minutes."

"Don't worry, Jennifer. I'll talk to him and fix this."

Jennifer didn't respond. She set her jaw. Her only movement was a flurry of rapid blinks to corral the mist forming in her eyes.

Concerned over Jennifer's fate and her abrupt change in demeanor, Emma finished breakfast in silence, wondering what she should do. Running out of time, she headed off to her first tutoring session back at the study in her quarters. Junior walked at her side.

"Is there any chance you could schedule a meeting with me and all the priests this afternoon?" Emma asked. "Perhaps at 1:00?"

"If I put out the request in your name, I can make it happen. May I suggest meeting in the auditorium?"

Emma didn't know that was an option. "Great idea."

Junior slowed his pace. "May I ask what you intend to do?"

"I want to talk to them directly and tell them what I've learned from the Sovereign." Emma brushed her hazel hair back from her face and looked at Junior. "Hopefully I can connect with them and let them know a little bit about me."

Junior chose his words with care. "Be aware that some priests will welcome this, others will be curious, and some will oppose you—a few quite vigorously."

"I also want to divide them into three groups."

"Toward what end?"

"I'm not sure, but I believe the Sovereign will reveal that to me at the time. Of that, I *am* sure."

4

ALPHA, BETA, GAMMA

The meeting with the tutor—which took place in the study inside Emma's quarters—lasted only a few minutes. The tutor had claimed the lone desk in the space. She outlined her plan while Emma stood, trying not to squirm in discomfort. "I'll have a folding table and chair here for you tomorrow to use as a desk. Then you'll have a place to do your lessons, which we'll begin tomorrow in earnest."

"Thank you." Even though Emma seethed inside, she wanted to show respect for the tutor.

The older woman kept Emma at a professional distance. She avoided eye contact and referred to Emma as "My Lord," which was how most people treated her and vexed her greatly. The woman never even shared her name.

They weren't off to a good start. For the first time in her life, Emma wasn't looking forward to learning.

With lunch now behind her—where Jennifer had also kept a reserved distance—Emma stood before the forty-eight priests. Pompous Jack was there too. She told them about her studying the Holy Text, of hearing supernatural insight, and of her spirit ascending into heaven to talk with the Sovereign.

Just as Junior had predicted, some priests received her words with excitement. Others seemed open to hear what she had to say but were hesitant to embrace it. The body language of the rest confirmed their antagonism toward her. Some sat with arms crossed, while others spent the time engaged with their smartphones. She doubted they heard a single word she said.

"I now want to divide you into three groups." This got everyone's attention. All eyes looked at her, but she still didn't know what she would do.

The Sovereign's instruction gave her the next step. *Search for auras.*

Emma scanned the priests as she peered into the spiritual realm. About one third of them had auras. This meant they had the Sovereign's Divine Spirit living within them. Knowing this thrilled her. They were her first group.

"I'm sorry. I don't know your names yet, so please forgive me for pointing." She then selected each priest with an aura. "You are in Gamma group. Please come back at 2:00 p.m., and we'll discuss the next step." She flashed them an excited look, but no one moved. "You may leave." Fifteen priests stood and left.

Search for colors, came the Sovereign's next instruction.

About half the remaining priests had a color in the spiritual realm. This meant they were spiritually open to move forward in their faith. Their potential also excited Emma. After pointing to each one, she announced, "You're in Beta group. Please come back at 3:00." With that, they left too.

The remaining priests looked at her with smug satisfaction. As they expected, Emma proclaimed they were in Alpha group. "Please come back at 4:00."

As they exited the room, Pompous Jack marched toward Emma. "I'm much too busy for your silly little meetings. My plate is full. So don't expect me to come back."

Emma had anticipated his opposition and was ready with an answer. "Perhaps you and I can meet in your office at 5:00. Then you can tell me about all you have on your full plate."

"I'll consider it." He stomped off.

Only Junior remained. "You didn't put me in any group." The hint of a smile danced on his lips. "Should I be concerned?"

Emma laughed. "You're in a class by yourself! You're the only inaugural member of Delta group, the best of the best. But I'd like your help as I meet with the other groups."

"Does that mean the groups are in reverse order from what most people would expect? If so, your selections are most astute. Though I'm not sure how you knew."

"The Sovereign revealed them to me." It was that simple.

As directed, Gamma group returned at 2:00. They were both punctual and expectant. This time, Emma stepped down from the stage to be on their level.

"I selected each of you because I perceive the Divine Spirit at work in your lives. You are the future of the priesthood here at the Temple. You will lead the other priests—and the people—into a new day."

Already receptive to what she would say, with this revelation they perked up even more. Their heads snapped up; their gaze riveted on her. Their faces beamed. A few wiped at the corner of their eyes. Without exception, Emma sensed no one had ever treated them this way. They were used to being secondary, of being overlooked, even dismissed. Now they would take the lead.

After proclaiming a blessing on them, they spent the rest of the hour discussing what their new role might look like and how Emma could help them move forward.

They left as Beta group arrived at 3:00.

"You've been disrespected as priests," Emma told them. "I plan to change that. You have much more to offer, and I want to help you reach your potential."

This lifted their perspectives. With renewed dignity, they discussed how they could grow in their faith and make a difference in the Temple and advance its work. As a group, their countenance lifted.

Emma ended with a prayer. "Sovereign Lord, bless these priests as they seek you. Help them grow in their faith and serve you more fully. May it be so." They left Emma's meeting talking with excitement over their renewed hope for their future at the Temple.

That left Alpha group. They trickled in around 4:00, fully expecting to receive Emma's confirmation for their high standing as the lead group.

Sovereign Lord, Emma whispered in her spirit. *Give me the right words to say. May I understand your perspective and clearly communicate it to them.*

As Emma scanned Alpha group, the Almighty's words flooded her mind, arriving like a mighty wave crashing on the shore. She cleared her throat to let them know she was ready to begin.

"This will be hard for you to hear," Emma said from her elevated position back on the stage, "but I call you Alpha group because you're the ones who need to do the most work to continue serving as priests here at the Temple."

Their complacency left them as fast as air escaping a deflated balloon. "I want you to succeed and be promoted to Beta group or even Gamma. First, you'll need to make changes and fix your attitude. I hope you'll all succeed at this, but if you don't want to try, then you best find a new job."

At that, the members of Alpha group stood and stomped out. They murmured as they did, throwing angry glances her way. The meeting had lasted a mere thirty seconds.

Having shared the Sovereign's words with them—and with her most difficult meeting over—relief flooded her being for completing her task as directed.

Yet an even harder one remained, her 5:00 with Pompous Jack.

5

CONFRONTATION

As the High Priestess, the Temple Palace was Emma's home, even though it repelled her. This implied that the office in the palace was hers as well, but Pompous Jack persisted in using it as his own. She'd need to put an end to that, but not today.

She prayed to the Sovereign for supernatural guidance. Nothing. She begged for the Almighty's protection.

Trust me, was all she heard. Then came silence.

As she and Junior arrived at the office, a young woman—one Emma had never seen before—scooted out. Pompous Jack was straightening his tie and didn't even glance up at them. "Sit down." He barked it as a command and not a courtesy.

There was only one chair. Emma sat while Junior remained standing. He squirmed, which did nothing to quell her throbbing heart.

Only then did Pompous Jack look up, fixing his gaze on Emma. "Here's your new schedule and my expectations: Your school day will begin at 8 a.m. sharp and go through to 5 p.m. You'll have a half hour for lunch and one mid-morning and one mid-afternoon break of fifteen minutes each. Is that clear?"

"What if I finish my classwork early?"

"You won't. I guarantee it."

Before she could protest, Pompous Jack continued.

"The rest of the time you're confined to quarters. The only exception is your appearance at the Sunday service. Aside from myself and your server, you'll have no interaction with any of the Temple staff. Is that clear?"

Emma stood so she could glare down at Pompous Jack. "You can't tell me what to do. I'm the High Priestess. You must do what I say."

Pompous Jack stood as well. At several inches taller, he seemed to tower over her. At least that's how it felt in this moment. He said, "Junior, leave us so that we may have a private discussion."

"You told me to never let her out of my sight. To always be with her."

"That assignment is now over, and I'll deal with your part in this rebel's little coup attempt later. Now I'm telling you to leave." Pompous Jack gave a dismissive flick of his hand. "Scat!"

Junior hesitated and then turned to leave.

"Shut the door behind you."

He did.

"Let me make the situation perfectly clear." Pompous Jack narrowed his gaze, as if to penetrate Emma's soul. "I'm in charge. You do what I tell you to do."

"The Holy Text says the High Priest is the leader of all."

"The Holy Text doesn't matter anymore. It's irrelevant. I've seen to that."

Emma struggled to stay calm. "If we don't use Scripture as the foundation for our faith, that means we can make it up as we go. A faith we've made up can't save us."

"I've been running the show for over twenty years, and you're not going to stop me now." He raised his eyebrows for emphasis.

"But I'm the head of the Temple."

"You are nothing more than a figurehead at

best, my simpleminded child. Besides, I'm the neck that turns the head." Pompous Jack snickered. "Never forget that. When the last High Priest opposed me on this, his time here came to an end."

"You killed him?" Emma's eyes popped open. "Are you threatening me too?"

"As I've already told you, I don't make threats. I make promises. Don't challenge me again, or it will be the last thing you do."

6

GUARDED

Emma stood there, as if frozen in time. She tapped her acting experience to remain calm on the outside, but inside she trembled.

Pompous Jack pushed a button on the desk phone and then looked at her. "Security will escort you to your quarters." A uniformed man strode into the office. He grabbed her arm just above the elbow and spun her toward the door, shoving her forward.

Junior wasn't there waiting for her. He was gone. She'd need to deal with this alone, without his support. It was just her. Well, her and the Sovereign. But if the Sovereign was with her, that was all the support she needed.

"Trust me," the Sovereign had said. Emma was

determined to do just that. She rolled her shoulders back and held her head high. She was the High Priestess, after all.

Twisting her arm free from the guard's grasp, she took a confident step forward and moved toward her quarters with intention. The man struggled to catch up and then matched her pace, but he didn't grab her arm again.

Reaching the door to her quarters, he opened it and shoved her inside. "A guard will be posted here, 24/7."

"Am I a prisoner?"

"If you need anything . . . don't ask me. Because I don't care."

Closing the door behind her, she headed straight to her bed and fell into it with an exhausted groan, not even bothering to change.

The phrase *confined to quarters* rifled through Emma's mind. She was a prisoner in her own home —albeit a home she didn't want. Yet it could be worse. Her quarters were spacious, with more square footage than a small house. Besides her expansive bedroom with ensuite bathroom—bright and airy—she had a sizable living room, a parlor, and a study. It also included a functional kitchenette and breakfast nook, along with a second smaller bedroom and bathroom. It also had a half bath for guests.

Even the smaller bedroom was likely larger than Junior's entire living space. She had no reason to complain. But the realization that—aside from the Sunday service—she would spend every moment in her quarters now made it feel like a prison. All that was missing were the bars.

She willed her mind to not think about it, and exhaustion overtook her. The next thing she knew, a tapping on the bedroom door interrupted her moment of morning slumber.

"Breakfast is served, My Lord."

Emma didn't recognize the voice. It certainly wasn't Jennifer, who had served her with excellence at every meal during the short time she had been High Priestess. With dawn sneaking through the curtains, Emma shuffled her way to the door and opened it just enough to peek. There stood an older woman. She wore a uniform like Jennifer's, but the detached look frozen on her face confirmed she was nothing like her younger counterpart.

"Breakfast is served, My Lord," the woman repeated. She scanned Emma from her head to her toes, most likely judging her for her disheveled hair and wrinkled clothes. "It'll be waiting for you in the parlor whenever you are ready."

"Now is fine." Emma trailed her to the parlor. "I haven't met you yet. What's your name?"

"I am here to serve you, but not to become your friend. His Royal Eminence was quite clear in that matter."

It figures that Pompous Jack was behind this. "Are we allowed to talk?"

"Only as it relates to my service for you. Anything more could cause me to receive a reprimand, which I prefer to avoid."

"I'm so sorry."

They reached the parlor, and there sat her breakfast, along with a single place setting.

"Where's Jennifer?"

"Effective immediately, she's on probation and will be reassigned . . . assuming she's reinstated. Regardless, going forward I will attend to your food service needs, just as I did for the last High Priest." The attendant pulled out the chair for Emma to sit and then eased it forward as she did.

Emma blessed the meal aloud. It tasted good, but not as good as Jennifer's food. It carried a subtle new flavor, one that Emma couldn't identify. She wasn't sure if she liked it or not, but an unpleasant aftertaste lingered.

As she ate, the attendant stood against the side wall, mute and staring straight ahead, with elbows out and fingers interlocked in front of her. She held that position until Emma finished eating. Only then did she speak.

"Your tutor awaits in your study." The attendant glanced at the wall clock. "Class begins in seven minutes. Don't be late."

7

———

THE TUTOR

Emma had just enough time to brush her teeth and use the bathroom before her lessons started. With fresh breath and renewed hope for the day, she breezed into the study two minutes early. Her tutor awaited.

"Good morning!" Emma wanted to start the day off right and make a good impression. She hoped yesterday's experience was an anomaly and today would go much better. Though Emma still didn't know the tutor's name, she felt this was not a good time to ask.

The tutor glanced at the time but said nothing. She did nothing.

As Emma squirmed in silence for two minutes, her mind recalled going to school, of the classes and teachers, of walking to school with Chloe and Joshua. Emma wished they were with her now. Though it seemed silly, she longed for Joshua's presence and for him to reach out and hold her hand. What comfort that would bring. *Oh Sovereign, be with Joshua—and Chloe too. Watch over them and keep them safe.*

At precisely 8:00, the tutor began class. "Since you missed your school assignments yesterday, you'll receive a double dose today to catch up. I expect you to accept this without complaint."

"Yes, ma'am. Can we do algebra first? It's my favorite subject."

Scowling, the tutor glanced at a paper on her desk. "Advanced algebra is your fifth period class. This is English. Please don't give me any grief about your schedule."

The tutor jotted something in a notebook. Once finished, she glanced Emma's way, but without making eye contact. "What are you waiting for?" she snapped. "Get going!"

"What am I supposed to do?" Emma shrugged.

"Are you daft? Or just belligerent!" The tutor made another notation in her book. "Read the next four chapters in *To Kill a Mockingbird*. Two for yesterday and two for today. Now not another peep out of you until second period history."

Unsure if she should say she understood or if that would be another peep, Emma kept quiet. She liked *To Kill a Mockingbird,* so much so that she had already read the next four chapters. Should she read them again or read further ahead?

Emma respected Atticus for his integrity and liked Scout for her youthful perspective and desire for justice. She identified with the bold girl on many levels.

Not wanting to incur any more of her tutor's wrath, Emma reread the four chapters. Not knowing what to do next, she continued reading, waiting for the class to end. Throughout this time, a low rumble of noise from people outside filtered in.

After an hour and twenty minutes, the tutor stood abruptly. "That concludes English class for today. We'll now begin second period history. Yesterday was review, and today is a test." She checked the time. "You have forty minutes to study and forty minutes to complete your exam."

"Yes, ma'am." Emma reviewed her notes for the material covered since the last test. She knew the content well but appreciated the opportunity to give it a final glance. After about twenty minutes, she felt more than ready.

With hesitation, she raised her hand. The tutor didn't acknowledge her. She cleared her throat. That didn't help. At last, she spoke. "I'm ready for the test."

The tutor glanced her way, giving a disapproving click of her tongue. "You have twenty more minutes to study. I suggest you use your time wisely." She looked down and made another entry in her notebook.

Twenty minutes later, the tutor handed Emma her history test. It was multiple choice, as Emma expected. She carefully read and answered every question. That took fifteen minutes. Then she reread every question and double-checked her answers. Everything looked good. That took five minutes more.

She didn't know if she should hand her test in early or sit in silence until the end of class. Not wanting to irritate her tutor's unspoken expectations, she pushed her test aside and laid her head on the desk, trying to make out the noises she heard from outside.

"That concludes history class," the tutor

announced loudly, jolting Emma from her daze. "You now have a 15-minute break."

Emma stood and handed her completed test to the tutor.

"What's this?"

"It's my history test."

"You should have turned it in during class. Now it's late." She grabbed the test from Emma, wrote a large F on it in red letters, and tossed it into the trash can. Then she left the room, leaving a shocked Emma in her wake.

Emma walked to the window in the study to peek outside and see what the commotion was all about. There was a protest happening in front of the Temple Palace. Several people carrying picket signs paraded in an elongated circle. Topher and Ashley walked side by side. Jennifer was there, too, along with five or six others. Their signs bore various messages, such as "More Pay," "Less Work," and "Increased Respect." Emma wished she could join them in their push for justice.

When she headed back to her seat, she noticed the tutor's notebook lying open on the desk. Though knowing she shouldn't read it, she did. The first line said, "Student is disrespectful." Below that was a column of other observations: "belligerent," "doesn't follow directions," "fails to manage time wisely," "disrespects authority," and "turns in assignments late."

Fuming, Emma returned to her desk and pulled out her laptop for computer science class. The day was not going as she had hoped. This may be the first time that she truly did not like school.

Third period didn't go any better. When she completed her assignment, she tabbed over to check email. Though she preferred texting, she still used email as needed. Her inbox overflowed with messages. But before she could read a single one, the tutor slammed the lid on her laptop shut. "This is not appropriate classroom behavior. You should know that! One demerit on your permanent record."

Emma snapped. "What are you going to write? That I misused technology?"

For the first time, the tutor almost smiled. "That's a good idea." She made another notation in her notebook.

The tutor gave Emma another assignment that would take the rest of the class. It was busy work, nothing more. Emma watched the minutes tick by. Finally, the tutor declared that computer science class was over.

That's when the food server made her announcement from the study doorway. "Lunch is served, My Lord."

Eager for a break and with her stomach rumbling with discontent, Emma stood to go to the parlor to eat lunch just as Pompous Jack glided in. He eyed the tutor and winked with a smirk. Then he glared at Emma. "Follow me."

Her heart thumped.

8

—————

A SHOCKING DEVELOPMENT

Pompous Jack led Emma out the back of the Temple Palace. He guided her toward the auditorium. The faint chant of the protesters wafted their way.

"More pay. Less work. Increased respect," they chanted. "More pay. Less work. Increased respect."

"This is all your fault," Pompous Jack said. "They were quite content until you arrived and stirred them up. I hold you accountable for their work slowdown."

"Slowdown?"

"They're not on strike, per se, but they're not doing their jobs either, at least not fully. They keep rotating in and out of their little march. Each time one ingrate arrives to join them, another one leaves to return to work. They put in just enough time to avoid dismissal." This clearly upset Pompous Jack.

"We need to help them," Emma said.

"What do you mean *we*?" Pompous Jack snorted. "You started this, and now I need to fix it. I should insist you repair the situation, but you'd only make matters worse."

"I agree with them and would like to join their protest."

"I'm quite sure you do, which is precisely why you're confined to quarters."

They arrived at the auditorium and walked inside. Junior awaited them. Emma wanted to run up and wrap her arms around him with a ginormous hug. Yet she knew that wouldn't help either of them. The best she could do was flash him a quick wink, which she hoped he interpreted as "It's good to see you, my friend."

Pompous Jack led them to the stage of the empty facility. He sat in the cathedra and motioned for Emma to take the diminutive chair next to him, the one she had sat in during last Sunday's service.

"Junior," he said. "Stand at the dais as though addressing a crowd." A large mat lay on the floor in front of the podium.

Junior moved to the spot.

Pompous Jack reached into the breast pocket of his designer suit and pulled out a small remote control. "Watch what happens when I push this button."

Junior turned around to see.

With a vicious gleam in his eyes, Pompous Jack pressed the control.

Junior shrieked and shook as he crumbled to the ground. His head thumped on the stage floor while his body writhed.

Emma screamed. "Junior!" She jumped up and rushed to his side. As his convulsions lessened, she turned to glare at Pompous Jack. "What did you do? Did you tase him or something?"

"Don't be silly, my simpleminded child."

Emma lay a comforting hand on Junior's shoulder. "It's going to be okay. I'm here and will protect you." His tremors slowly ebbed.

Pompous Jack smirked. "I merely demonstrated what I will do to you if you don't cooperate during next Sunday's service."

"You wouldn't dare. Not in front of the people and on national TV."

Pompous Jack crossed his arms. A playful smile danced on his lips. "I'd merely explain that the Sovereign had disciplined you for trying to become

High Priestess. End of story. End of Emma Barlow."

Returning her attention to Junior, Emma moved her hand from his shoulder and placed it on his forehead. "Sovereign Lord, restore Junior to full health, just as you did through the prophets of old in the Holy Text. May he have no side effects from this and have a full recovery. Amen."

Junior's eyes fluttered as his gaze flitted her way. "Thank you," he mouthed. "I'm going to be all right," he said. "Though it will take a few minutes before I can stand." Then he added in a whisper, "Be careful with what you say and do."

Emma brushed Junior's cheek with the back of her hand. "I will," she whispered. "You do the same."

"Like he said, he's going to be okay." Pompous Jack said this with authority, but then he lowered his voice and mumbled, "at least I think so."

His uncertainty heightened Emma's concern for Junior even more.

"Hop to it, young lady." Pompous Jack snapped his fingers. "You best hustle back to school before you're late."

Emma gave Junior a concerned glance, and he nodded his approval for her to leave.

Even though she didn't want to abandon her friend, Emma slowly turned away, but not before mouthing the word "Sorry" to him. She strode to the main doors of the auditorium. Once outside, the distant chant of the protesters reached her ears.

"More pay. Less work. Increased respect."

Excitement rushed through her. She broke into a jog to return to class at the palace.

Out of breath, she burst through the doorway of the study just as the tutor announced the beginning of art class. "Let me grab my lunch, and I'll be right back."

"Your lunch break is over. It's not my fault you squandered that time. I suggest you sit down immediately for class, or else I'll have no option but to assign you detention."

"Detention? When will we squeeze that in? I'm already stuck here until five." Only after it was too late did Emma realize she shouldn't have said that last bit. It would surely earn her another note in the teacher's log.

"Detention will be from 6:00 p.m. until 9:00. You're this close to receiving it." The tutor held up her hand with her thumb and index finger about two inches apart and slowly brought them together.

"That's okay." Emma sat down. "Let's do art."

That's when she noticed the empty spot on her workspace. "Where's my laptop?"

"I confiscated it because of your persistence in using it during class."

"It's my personal property. Give it back."

"His Royal Eminence made it perfectly clear to me that I have complete authority over what happens during your school day."

"How am I supposed to do my work without a computer?"

"You should have thought of that before you misused it. You'll need to do everything with pen and paper from now on."

"Even for computer science? How's that going to work?"

"Going forward, your computer science class will focus on theory and not application. The same applies to art. Today you have a documentary about the Renaissance period." The tutor fingered a remote control, and the TV mounted on the wall to Emma's right flickered on. A video played. She turned her folding chair to face it.

After art came Advanced Algebra and then a break. Emma dashed to the parlor, hoping her lunch was still there. She gobbled as much as she could stomach, but it tasted odd and rumbled in her gut. With her head spinning, she returned to the study just in time for AP bio, her last class of the day. Again, the focus would be on theory with no lab, which was usually her favorite part of biology. Emma spent the entire period reading through the assigned text.

At last, the tutor stood. "That concludes school for today. I suggest you return tomorrow with a renewed attitude and be better prepared to complete your assignments without all the drama." With that, the tutor picked up Emma's laptop and clomped away. Only when Emma heard the door to her quarters shut did she release a long sigh. Her shoulders drooped.

At last, she was alone, but she wasn't treated to silence. Instead, the chants of the protesters outside became clearer. She walked to the window to see what was happening.

9

___

PROTESTING

The protesters continued their chant. "More pay. Less work. Increased respect." Jennifer was still there—apparently because she no longer had a job to return to—and seven other Temple employees had joined her, replacing the earlier group. "More pay. Less work. Increased respect."

A TV remote truck sped in and came to an abrupt stop before the picketers. A reporter jumped out and ran up to Jennifer, striding at her side with microphone in hand, attempting to capture an interesting sound bite for the evening news.

Pompous Jack dashed up too. He attempted to intervene. The camera operator captured his actions, which would no doubt be used to reveal his obstruction of a peaceful protest.

Emma tried to open the window so she could hear better. It didn't budge. It probably hadn't been opened in years. She banged on the frame with the base of her palm, hoping to dislodge it. On her third try, the frame creaked. When she tugged on it again, it shuddered open. A cool breeze rushed into the stuffy room. With a grunt, she shoved the window fully open and stuck her head outside.

Pompous Jack took a step back from the protesters. He held up his hands to show he wouldn't interfere. The reporter rushed toward him and thrust a microphone in front of his face.

"I appreciate you for sharing your concerns." His best smile erupted on his normally dour face. "Now that you've brought these issues to my attention, I'll make it my top priority to look into the situation and address it."

The protestors stopped marching. Several lowered their signs.

"Please return to your normal duties, with no fear of reprisals. I give you my word."

The protesters looked at Jennifer, and Pompous Jack followed their gaze. "You can have your job back too." That's when she lowered her sign, the last to do so. As a group, the eight protesters slunk away.

Yet Emma knew Pompous Jack wouldn't follow through. His pledge was a ruse—nothing more. She knew him well enough to know that he couldn't be trusted. She couldn't allow him to come across as the hero to a problem he had made.

Emma took a deep breath. "More pay. Less work. Increased respect." She belted it out. "More pay. Less work. Increased respect."

The camera operator pivoted her way and zoomed up to her high vantage point in the palace. "More pay. Less work. Increased respect."

This also garnered the attention of the retreating protesters. They turned around to watch her too.

"More pay. Less work. Increased respect." Emma wasn't sure what to do next. How long could she keep this up on her own? For the sake of all the Temple employees, she needed to not let Pompous Jack dismiss their plight.

As she paused to take her next breath, she heard the reporter say, "The High Priestess is siding with the protesters."

Emma thrust her fist in the air and shouted even

louder. "More pay. Less work. Increased respect." She filled her lungs again. "More pay. Less—"

A firm hand grabbed her shoulder and spun her around. She thudded to the floor, which forced all the air from her lungs.

Dazed, Emma looked up to see a man from Pompous Jack's private security detail standing over her. He was the same one who had stood guard at her residence door yesterday. "Will you ever learn to stop causing trouble?"

"Help!" But with no air left in her lungs to propel her plea, the word came out as a mere whisper.

Before she could try again, the security guard was on top of her. With his hand clamped over her mouth, his full weight rested on her torso. Emma had always been a fighter, but so far her battles had been verbal and not physical.

A primal rage rose inside of her, and she flailed her arms at his face. Her hand contacted his cheek. She shoved her nails into his face and drug them across his flesh, producing four dark red lines along their path.

"You little witch!" He drew back his hand and slapped her cheek with full force. Still tender from when the SWAT officer had hit her last week, a jolt of pain assaulted her. At that time, she had tried to stop Joshua's arrest. Now it seemed like a life and death battle—hers. She must prevail . . . somehow.

The follow-through of his slap left him positioned to execute a second blow as he brought the back of his hand to her other cheek. His knuckles made contact, and her cheekbone cracked. Shooting pain ricocheted inside her head. Though she surmised the SWAT officer had broken her cheek last week, she was sure this man broke her other cheek now.

"Help!" This time the word came out with more intensity, but she wasn't sure if it was loud enough for anyone to hear. Perhaps the reporter still watched from outside. Maybe the protesters had heard and would rush to her aid.

Before she could make another attempt to call out, the guard yanked a leather glove from his belt and jammed it into her mouth. Then he grabbed her right arm and pinned it underneath his knee. He repeated the process with her left arm. She couldn't scream, and she couldn't flail her arms, but she could still move her legs.

She kneed him in his back, but it had little impact. She tried a second time with as much force as possible but accomplished nothing more than provoking a slight irritation. Kneeing him wasn't helping. What if she could swing her entire leg high enough to hook his shoulder and force him to the side? Then she might be able to escape.

Emma rocked her leg up exactly as envisioned. She did indeed catch his shoulder with her calf and spun him away. As he tottered, he grabbed her shoulder and flipped her over, leaving her face down on the floor. Before she knew what had happened, he grabbed her arm and pulled it to her back. He cuffed one wrist and then the other, ratcheting it shut with an alarming click.

He stood. "That was a nice little workout you gave me. I almost broke a sweat." Though Emma couldn't see his face, his tone seemed quite pleased. He grabbed her upper arm and jerked her to her feet. Both cheekbones throbbed and her head spun.

The guard shoved her forward, propelling her from the study and toward her bedroom. She stumbled a few times and almost fell once. As they neared her bed, he gave her a last violent thrust. Emma tumbled forward with a grunt, mostly landing on her bed. He turned off the lights and slammed the door shut, leaving her in complete darkness.

The immediate threat was gone, and she was

safe for the moment. *Thank you, Sovereign, for being with me and saving my life.*

With effort, she shimmied her way to a less uncomfortable position on the bed. She reviewed her situation. Her arms were cuffed behind her back. His leather glove remained stuffed in her mouth, and her jaw ached from being forced open wider than normal. Both cheekbones throbbed, and her head pounded. Oh, one more thing, she had to pee.

Using her tongue, she tried to push the glove out of her mouth. It wouldn't budge. Next, she rubbed the lump of leather against the mattress, trying to dislodge it by twisting her head. That didn't work either. If only she could get her hands in front of her instead of behind, then she could pull the glove out of her mouth. Maybe she should focus on that first.

She'd heard of people being cuffed in back and able to reposition the restraints to their front, but she didn't know how. Her arms were long. That might work in her favor. She twisted her body; she shimmied and contorted. With painful effort, she labored to maneuver her cuffed wrists past her butt. That left her body doubled over and the cuffs behind her knees. She had traded one uncomfortable position for another. That's when her left thigh cramped. She needed to do something and do it fast!

Someone tapped on her bedroom door. "Dinner is served, My Lord."

Emma tried to coax a groan for help from her dammed-up mouth but doubted the server could hear her pitiful attempt.

Silence.

She tried again, but with no more volume.

There were several more seconds of silence. "It's in the parlor, My Lord. I'll leave it there for whenever you're ready."

Desperate to free herself, Emma resolved to do whatever it took. With a grimace, she freed one leg, leaving her in an even more precarious position. She fought back panic and braced for more pain as she twisted her second leg free. At last, her cuffs were before her, but not without a cost. She had twisted one knee and badly scraped her other ankle. She suspected it was bleeding, but being in the dark, she couldn't see how badly. Her thigh still throbbed, and she had strained both shoulders.

With the increased ability to move, she pulled the glove from her mouth and massaged the joints on either side of her jaw to rub in some relief. Then she wiped away the tears of pain that had leaked from her eyes. In a few minutes, her breathing returned to normal. The exhale of each breath brought a bit more relief.

She rolled off the bed and turned on the lights. Yes, her searing ankle was bleeding, but not as badly as she had feared. She then used the bathroom. She had now addressed her immediate concerns. *If only I could remove these cuffs*, she thought.

Just lift your hands, came the Sovereign's quick reply.

As Emma did, both cuffs released in tandem and fell to the ground. This was exactly what had happened in the police van after they'd arrested her last week.

You could have done that sooner. Even though it sounded sarcastic, Emma meant it as humor, grateful that her predicament was now much less than what it had been.

Never ask me to do what you can accomplish yourself, came the Sovereign's reply. *Handle what you can, and trust me with the rest.*

I will, Emma thought. *Promise.*

10

FOGGY

Emma gingerly touched her throbbing right cheek. It radiated warmth. Pain shot from it. Surely, it was broken. Her left cheek hurt too. She washed her bleeding ankle and stopped the flow. It would be okay. So would her jaw, shoulders, and thigh, but they might ache for a few days.

She limped to the parlor and considered her supper. It smelled good; it looked good, but something tasted a bit off. Suspecting that food would help speed her recovery, Emma forced herself to eat everything in front of her, even though she didn't want to. As she ate, her stomach protested and knotted inside. When the cramps became unbearable, she shoved the rest of the food aside.

She pulled out her phone to text Junior. She wanted to make sure he was okay and update him so he wouldn't worry about her, but something was wrong with her phone. It had bars but wouldn't work. The display said something about needing to activate it.

Did Pompous Jack turn off my phone? How could he even do such a thing?

Though she couldn't text, call, or check email, all the basic functions remained. The time displayed, she could take pictures, and her calendar was still there. She could do everything but communicate. Not helpful. Worthless, in fact. She jammed the device into her pocket.

Emma shuffled to her room with an uncontrollable urge to sleep, even though bedtime was several hours away. She felt lost without her laptop and a bit displaced knowing she couldn't use her phone. At least she could study the Holy Text.

Except she couldn't.

It wasn't where she had left it. Her notebook was missing too. Anger surged within her, a righteous indignation. Though she could replace her copy of the Holy Text, her months of insights recorded in her notebook were irreplaceable. She had no backup of all she'd learned since she began her quest.

Oh, Sovereign. What am I to do?

Your notebook is not lost. The Sovereign's words reassured Emma. *Pompous Jack has it locked in his desk drawer. You will one day be able to retrieve it. Until then, trust me. Seek me.*

Having the Sovereign use her nickname for the man surprised Emma, even though the Sovereign was omniscient and knew all things.

The Sovereign continued. *I giggle every time you call him Pompous Jack. That so delights me. It confirms you share my perspective.*

It was hard for Emma to imagine the Sovereign giggling, which made her giggle too.

Emma determined to do just as instructed and seek the Sovereign. She lay on her bed and stretched her arms heavenward. *Oh Sovereign. Receive my spirit in the spiritual realm. May I bask in your presence and be refreshed.*

Nothing happened. Emma waited. She repeated her petition. Still nothing. Surely, she could seek an audience with the Sovereign just as easily from her bed as from the Temple floor. Right?

She sang some of her favorite hymns and

recited verses from the Holy Text. She fell asleep mid passage.

The next thing she knew, her alarm signaled it was time to get up. She didn't want to. Though she always started her day with difficulty, today was worse. Much worse. Her mind was foggy. Despite sleeping for nearly thirteen hours, she had no energy.

A gentle tap on her bedroom door brought her back to reality. "Breakfast is served, My Lord."

"I'm not feeling well. I'm not sure I can make it."

"Should I fetch it," came a hesitant reply, "and serve you in bed?"

"Please." With that, Emma drifted back to sleep.

The server shook Emma's shoulder. "You must eat, My Lord."

Emma's eyes flittered open. With effort, she repositioned herself on the bed, propped up by some pillows and leaning against the headboard. With the server's help, she ate a few nibbles of toast but couldn't tolerate any more. Her stomach roiled.

Look at your food, the Sovereign said.

Emma did.

Don't fix your eyes on what is seen but what is unseen.

What do you mean?

See through your spirit.

Emma closed her eyes and reached out with her spirit to study the food. She gasped. What looked delicious and appealing in the physical world was rancid and disgusting in the spiritual.

You're being poisoned, the Sovereign said. *It's killing you. Don't eat another bite.*

It all made sense now.

It's how the last High Priest died, the Sovereign added.

Emma realized she might be next. This explained why her last several meals had tasted a bit off and squeezed her gut like a vise. This is why she was so tired. This is why she couldn't focus.

"I can't eat another bite." Emma wasn't sure if the server knew the food was tainted or not. What Emma did know was to keep this new knowledge to herself. "Thank you for breakfast," Emma said, "but I'm not hungry. You may take it away. Maybe my appetite will return at lunch." But Emma knew she wouldn't eat a bite of it.

It was almost 8:00 and time for school. As the server left, Emma shuffled along behind her, still wearing her clothes from yesterday and having not taken a shower. Yet to be late would surely result in another notation in the tutor's notebook, a demerit on her permanent record, or detention. Possibly all three. Emma couldn't risk it.

She plopped into her chair with a thump.

The tutor gave her a questioning look, making eye contact for the first time. "It seems you failed to follow my recommendations from yesterday, just as I feared you would. His Royal Eminence told me you were nothing more than a troubled teenager with a massive savior complex. You're nothing but a fraud. I can see that now and will treat you appropriately."

Jumbled thoughts swirled in Emma's unfocused mind. She was too tired to react. She was even too tired to hold her head up, so she rested it on her desk.

"English class begins now."

The next thing she knew, it was morning break. She shuffled back to her room and fell into bed.

Oh, Sovereign. Protect me from this poison so I may live another day.

11

______

DUMBWAITER

Emma woke to the sun's rays shooting through a crack in the heavy drapes. *Is it morning? Did I miss a whole day?*

Her mind scrambled to make sense of her situation. She scrutinized the beam of light. There was something odd about it. The angle was wrong. The morning sun should come from the left of her window and shine to the right. This ray pointed the opposite way, so the sun was setting. It must be evening. She'd only slept for about twelve hours and not a full day.

Though weak from not eating, she wasn't as dizzy, and her stomach no longer cramped. Overall, she felt better, at least marginally so. Still, Emma struggled to stand. After teetering for several seconds, she shuffled to the parlor. She hoped food would await her, only to remember it might be poisoned.

It looked good to her eyes, but her spirit revealed she shouldn't eat it, perhaps even more so than before, given its darker color and the smoke that puffed from it in the spiritual realm.

She knew a person could go several days without food, but water was more essential. *Was the water also poisoned?*

She turned on the tap in the kitchenette and analyzed the water through her spirit. Given its supernatural color and smell, she knew it wasn't safe. The same proved true from the water in the bathroom sink. *What about the shower?*

It flowed crisp and clear to both her eyes and her spirit. She drank as much as she could and filled a pitcher with more. Water, she thought, might help wash the poison from her body. She resolved to drink as much as she could, wondering if it might also stave off her hunger pains.

It was a short-term solution, but she still needed to find some safe food. Running out of ideas, she felt she had done all she could. It was time to seek divine help. *Sovereign Lord,* she prayed in her spirit. *Show me where to find food.*

Check out the portrait of the former High Priest in the parlor.

Looking at a painting seemed like an odd instruction, but Emma obeyed. She saw no food. What was she expecting, anyway?

She studied its frame and its mount. It didn't hang like most pictures but had hidden hinges on one side. It swung away with ease.

Behind it was an opening in the wall, which the oversized portrait smartly covered. A rope looped over a pulley above the opening and dropped into a dark shaft below. *Is it a tiny elevator?*

A plaque simply read, "Dumbwaiter load limit 200 lbs." To the right was an unlabeled button.

Retrieving her phone, she turned on its light and peered down the shaft. It certainly looked like a small elevator.

She pushed the button, and the rope moved. Resting her hand on the wall, she felt a slight vibration. After about ten seconds, a box rose into view. Aside from a couple of dusty plates and some tarnished silverware, its three shelves were otherwise empty.

Wondering what to do, she pressed the button again. The vibration came back, and the compart ment sunk from view. After about ten seconds, the vibration stopped.

Pushing the button a third time, the compartment returned.

She propped up her phone in the back of the dumbwaiter and set it to record a video. She pushed the dumbwaiter button and watched the compartment disappear. Fifteen seconds later, she pressed the control again, and the dumbwaiter returned. The video revealed another door at the bottom of the shaft.

Emma tried to recall the layout of the floor below. She wondered if the smaller of the two kitchens was below the parlor. If so, perhaps the dumbwaiter was a way to speed food to her quarters.

She also wondered if it was her way of escape.

Removing its contents and the shelves, Emma studied the space before her. Could she fold her body to fit inside that box? Could she keep her claustrophobia in check long enough to make the ten-second trek? What if the door at the bottom didn't open? Was she stuck there, or could she return?

She sat on the floor of the dumbwaiter and edged back. She rolled her shoulders forward and tipped her head down to duck inside. It wasn't comfortable, but at least the top part of her fit. She pulled in one leg and jammed her foot into the back corner. Only one leg remained.

She could get her foot in, but not her knee. Or her knee would fit, but then her foot stuck out. She twisted and contorted and nearly corralled her entire frame inside the cramped space. But panic overtook her, and she tumbled out in a heart-pounding gasp, crashing on the floor.

For the next thirty minutes, she attempted to twist her body to conform to the too-small space.

Giving up, she went to Plan B.

If the dumbwaiter wasn't a way for her to escape, maybe it was a way for Junior to send her some food.

Though she had so far only connected with Gabe in the spiritual realm, she suspected she could reach out to Junior as well. She found his spirit easily enough and roused his attention. But her supernatural presence confused him, and she couldn't communicate.

Next, she tried her mentor.

Gabe, are you there?

I am most delighted to hear from you and am relieved to know you are surviving your travail.

Emma didn't know what travail meant, but it sounded like the right word to explain what she had been going through. *Can you get a message to Junior?*

I suggest the more expedient option would be for you to send him one of your text messages.

My phone's disabled, Emma said through her spirit, *and I have no way to communicate with anyone except supernaturally with you.*

In that case, I am ready and able to assist.

Emma told him about the dumbwaiter and her need for food.

I have just acquired one of these modern communication devices, Gabe said in his spirit, *and am seeking to master its operation. I will compile an appropriate communiqué to update the priest called Junior of your situation and dispatch it to him, posthaste.*

Though Emma trusted Gabe completely and he had never let her down, for the first time, she doubted his ability to follow through. All she could do now was wait.

But she didn't need to wait long.

Minutes later, the dumbwaiter dropped from view and soon reappeared with random pieces of food: a dinner roll, a fried chicken breast, an apple, a chef salad, and a frosted brownie. Examining them with her spirit, Emma saw that each one was safe to eat.

She had removed everything except the brownie when the dumbwaiter dropped from sight. It soon returned with the brownie, a pad of paper, and a pen, along with a hastily written question, "Do you need a replacement cell phone?"

YES! Emma scribbled. She returned the elevator to Junior, but not before grabbing her brownie.

In no time at all, the dumbwaiter returned, but it didn't carry the cell phone she expected. Instead, it delivered something even better.

12

SURPRISE!

As the dumbwaiter rose into view, a person rose with it. Her black hair appeared first. Could it be?

"Chloe!" Emma rushed forward as her best friend appeared.

Before the dumbwaiter eased to a stop, Chloe tumbled out. "That was intense!" Picking herself up, Chloe surveyed her friend with a critical gaze. "You okay?"

"Much better, now that you're here." Emma pushed her tangled hair away from her face.

"That's quite a shiner you have." Chloe lifted her hand toward Emma's cheek but stopped short of touching it. "How bad does it hurt?"

"Bad. Really bad. I think he broke my cheekbone."

"Why don't you just heal it, like you did the other week with the gash on your head?"

"I didn't heal it. The Sovereign did."

"So why didn't the Sovereign heal it this time?"

Emma's shoulders sagged and her gaze dropped to the floor. "Because I never thought to ask." She closed her eyes and corralled her thoughts. Once she focused her spirit on the Sovereign, she lifted her hand to her tender cheek and prayed. "Oh, Sovereign Lord, heal my cheek. Take away the pain. In your name and for your glory. So be it." As she released her breath, the pain ebbed and soon went away. "That feels much better. Thanks for reminding me of the obvious."

"The pain's gone?" Chloe seemed doubtful. "Your eye's still black."

Emma moved her hand to her eye. "Sovereign Lord, take away the bruise on my face. Amen."

Chloe shook her head. "Looks the same. Why didn't the Sovereign answer that prayer too?"

Emma also wondered. "I'm sure the Sovereign has a reason, but the pain is gone. That's what matters most."

Chloe seemed doubtful. "No offense, but you look like death warmed over."

"That's kind of how I feel. All I want to do is sleep. I'm not sure when I last changed clothes, let alone had enough energy to shower." Emma blinked, trying to control the pent-up emotions that threatened to erupt now that she was with her best friend. She extended her arms. "I probably stink, but . . . Hug?"

Chloe rushed forward and wrapped her arms around Emma, pulling her into a tight embrace.

That's when Emma's tears unleashed. "They're trying to kill me."

Chloe pulled back and looked up at her friend. "Oh?"

Emma tipped her head toward the tray of tainted supper. "It's toxic."

"That's why you asked Junior for food?"

"I haven't eaten all day, and what I had yesterday filled my body with poison. I think I almost died."

"We didn't know how bad things were for you," Chloe said. "But Junior thought you might like my company while he and Topher went out to get you a prepaid phone."

"I'm so glad you came."

"Me too." Then Chloe shuddered. "It was a tight fit in the dumbwaiter, and I don't think I have it in me to go back the same way."

"I tried to climb in myself," Emma said, "but I just couldn't do it. Besides not fitting, I don't like tight places. I'd likely have panicked and freaked out about halfway down."

Chloe scanned Emma's tall frame. "If I barely fit, surely you never would. I'm glad you didn't force it."

Emma nodded. She wiped her face with the back of her hand and strode toward the food that Junior had sent. She raised her arms heavenward. "Thank you, Sovereign, for answering my prayer, for food, and for good friends." With that, she began scarfing down her meal.

Chloe drew a cup of water from the kitchen faucet and brought it to Emma.

Emma shook her head. "It's poisoned too."

Chloe held up the glass of clear liquid to examine it. "How do you know?"

"My spirit can see what my eyes cannot." That was the best explanation Emma could offer.

"Do you think I could learn to do that? Will you teach me?"

"I could try, but I think Gabe is your best

option. He taught me how to do it last week. Though I'm getting better, I still have a lot to learn."

"Maybe I'll ask him," Chloe said. "I'm not so scared of him anymore. It's strange, but I kind of feel drawn to him now."

"I'm sure he'd help you. He's helped me and Joshua."

"Speaking of Joshua," Chloe said with a teasing smile, "you're all he's been talking about the last two days. Without you, he's like a little lost puppy."

"I've been thinking a lot about him too."

"That's good, because he's worried you'll forget about him."

"Not a chance. We're soulmates! One day we'll get married."

"Oh?" Chloe looked up to stare at her friend. "Seriously? How long have you known?"

Emma laughed. "About five seconds. The Sovereign just revealed it to me."

"Then he doesn't know about your 'engagement'?" Chloe made air quotes around the word engagement.

Emma shrugged. "I think he might know, but we haven't talked about it. Besides, that's a long way off. We're only fifteen."

Emma left to retrieve the pitcher of safe drinking water. She felt better already. The food helped, but she knew in her spirit that she wasn't yet out of danger.

"Though it's only been three days," Emma said, "it feels like I haven't seen you in, like, forever. Are things going better at school, now that I'm not there to be a 'distraction'?" Now it was Emma's turn to make air quotes.

Chloe lowered her gaze. "No."

"Why?"

"Now that they don't have you to harass, they've turned their attention to Joshua and me, along with the rest of our group."

"So sorry. I was sure that once I left, things would return to normal."

"We're not safe there. Principal Johnson won't do anything to help. He just keeps saying that his hands are tied."

"I suspect that's true." Emma sensed Pompous Jack was involved and likely giving orders to the otherwise conscientious principal.

"Joshua said his mother will change her work schedule next week and start homeschooling him. My dad's looking into distance learning for me. Same with Lane." Chloe's face brightened when she said his name. "I'm not sure about the rest of our group, but none of us want to be at school anymore."

With her food gone, Emma refilled her glass with water from the pitcher. "Let's hang out in the living room." Emma gestured for Chloe to go first, but when she didn't move, Emma realized her friend had no clue where the living room was. "Let me give you a tour."

As they walked from room to room, Chloe oohed and aahed over the decor and opulence. "I think you have more space here than we do in our entire house."

"Sorry."

"Don't be sorry. My dad and I have plenty of room. It's just that . . . it looks like you have too much."

"Junior says the room next to his in the priests' quarters is open. I was thinking about moving there, but later. Right now, I have bigger issues to deal with."

"We saw you on the news the other night. The whole country did. Probably the world."

"The TVs here aren't receiving a signal. And my tutor took my laptop. So, without my phone, I have no idea what's going on."

"They called you a hero, siding with the protesters and all. On the news, we watched the video of a man grab you from behind and pull you away from the window. The rest of the report was all speculation."

"They don't know who did it?"

"Though the Prime Minister is yet to condemn what happened, the Senate has launched a probe. But it will take months to finish their investigation. The good news is Captain Hernandez is looking into it too. He texted you and Joshua . . . but since your phone isn't working, I guess you don't know that."

"I was hoping they'd have arrested the guy who assaulted me by now." Emma let out a dejected sigh.

Chloe stood. "Let me get my phone and text Joshua for an update."

Fighting off fatigue, Emma couldn't think of anything to say and merely nodded.

Chloe returned empty-handed. "It's gone! I laid it on the dumbwaiter floor when I climbed in. But the dumbwaiter isn't there, and the button isn't working. I think I'm stuck here."

"Then I guess we're having a sleepover," Emma

said. "We'll deal with the dumbwaiter problem in the morning."

"Agreed."

"What about your dad? He'll be worried."

"He's out of town on a business trip. So, it's all good."

Though Emma lacked the energy, Chloe talked her into taking a shower, washing her hair, and putting on clean clothes. It zapped what little strength she had left, but she felt better for it. During that time, Chloe had picked up the parlor, living room, and kitchenette to remove any hint that Emma had a guest. Then the pair retreated to the bedroom.

Before they drifted off to sleep, Emma prayed. "Sovereign, thank you for sending Chloe to me. Give us wisdom on what to do tomorrow so she can leave. Oh, and it would be nice for some food in the morning to feed my guest."

13

———

FOOD AND FLIGHT

The next thing Emma knew, it was morning. She didn't want to get up, as was usually the case. With a moan, she rolled over to return to her slumber. That's when she noticed Chloe wasn't there. *Did she leave?*

She allowed her eyes to flutter closed and let sleep overtake her. It did.

"Emma." Chloe's gentle voice bathed Emma's ears. "Emma, you need to get up." A hand brushed Emma's shoulder. "We're burning daylight, girlfriend."

"What time is it?" Emma croaked.

"Ten thirty." Chloe opened the drapes in the room's lone window, and sunshine flooded the space. Emma raised a hand to shield her eyes.

"Your breakfast was delivered hours ago and is sitting in the parlor."

Emma's eyes popped open. "You didn't eat any of it, did you?"

"Of course not. But I sure am hungry."

Emma sat up in bed and extended her hand toward Chloe. "Let's take a step of faith."

Chloe hesitated for a moment and then reached out to take Emma's hand. "Okay."

"Almighty Lord," Emma prayed, as she lifted her other hand heavenward. "We thank you for the food that you have provided and which we're about to enjoy. May it give us strength for the day ahead. Amen."

Chloe released Emma's hand. "Now what?"

"Let's explore." Emma left the room, with Chloe trailing behind.

The kitchenette, the Sovereign said to Emma.

Emma led Chloe there.

The mini fridge, the Sovereign said to Emma.

Emma tipped her head toward the refrigerator. "I think we'll find breakfast in there."

Chloe gave Emma a questioning look. "It's empty. I already checked."

"Check again."

Chloe did and gasped. "There's a whole day's

worth of food, enough for us both. How did that happen? A half hour ago it was bare."

Emma bowed her head and lifted her hands. "Thank you, Sovereign, for providing our food for today."

"It's like our daily bread!" Chloe confirmed this with a decided downward tip of her head.

Retreating to the living room, Emma explained what she had learned about the Sovereign, faith, and moving in the supernatural. Chloe sucked it all in like a hungry hoover, inhaling everything Emma said. "Will you teach me how to see into the spiritual realm?"

"I'll try," Emma said, "but don't get your hopes up. I still think Gabe is the best one to teach you, but since he's not here, you're stuck with me."

"I'm ready."

The pair sat on the floor facing each other. Emma extended both hands to Chloe. Trembling, Chloe grabbed them. "I'm nervous," she said, "but I'm kind of excited too."

"Close your eyes," Emma coached her friend. "Almighty Sovereign," she prayed, "I ask you to open Chloe's eyes in the spiritual realm so she can see you and all the wonders in store for her there."

"No!" Chloe shrieked, clutching Emma's hands tightly.

Emma squeezed back even harder. "I'm here. Whatever you do, don't let go. Don't give up. Just breathe . . . Tell me what you see."

"I see darkness. We're surrounded by black." Chloe's voice shook. "Evil is all around. Terrifying creatures fly about. They want to hurt us."

"But they're not, are they? The Sovereign is protecting us, keeping us safe. We have nothing to fear. Do you see anything else?"

"There's a white glow coming from you. Really bright. The creatures fear it."

"What about you?" Emma asked.

"Not as bright, but a soft green light comes from me. I think the creatures are afraid of it too."

"The Sovereign is protecting us, but I can't say the same for my quarters. We need to claim it as a sanctified place, with no room for evil."

"How do we do that?"

"I'm not sure." Emma breathed slowly as she awaited direction from the Sovereign. Yet the Almighty remained silent, which Emma took as confirmation that she knew enough to move forward on her own.

"Join me in prayer," Emma said to her friend. "Agree with me in your spirit."

"I have no idea how to do that."

Emma prayed. "Lord, we give this space to you, my entire quarters. Consecrate it and make it holy. Keep evil from entering." The light from Emma and Chloe's essences expanded, pushing away the darkness that encircled them. "Put a protective hedge around my quarters. May it repel all spirits—and all people—who don't align with you. May it be so."

"Amen," came the simple agreement from Chloe.

With that last statement, all black vanished, as if silently sucked out by a supernatural vacuum. What remained was pure, holy . . . and safe.

The girls opened their eyes and released their vise-like grip of each other.

"Is it always like this?" Chloe asked.

"No. I forgot what a dark place this was. I've learned to tune it out, but I wasn't thinking about how bad it would freak you out. Please forgive me. I'm sorry."

"You mean that seeing into the spiritual realm is usually less scary?"

"Most definitely."

A noise interrupted their discussion. The main door of the High Priest's quarters creaked open. The food server let out a terrified shriek. A tray of food clattered to the floor.

"We can't let her see you!" Emma whispered to Chloe. "Hide." Tiptoeing, Emma led Chloe into the spare bedroom. The food server would have no reason to go in there.

Hiding behind the bed, they heard a hurried flurry of activity in the parlor. Within seconds, the woman made a hasty retreat.

"Your food is in the parlor, My Lord," the food server called out, much louder and more urgent than usual. She slammed the main door shut.

"Wow, that was close," Chloe said. "What in the world was that all about?"

"Remember our prayer to sanctify my quarters? We prayed that this space would repel everything not aligned with the Sovereign. It certainly seems to have done the trick with the food server."

"Does that mean she's evil?"

"She is trying to poison me, after all," Emma said. "That's how the last High Priest died."

"Seriously?"

"Yep! The Sovereign told me."

The pair headed to the kitchenette to retrieve

their lunch from the mini fridge. They sat in the breakfast nook to eat their next meal and discuss what happened. The conversation lasted until late afternoon, when Emma suggested they retreat to the bedroom before the food server returned with dinner, assuming she came back at all.

Right at five, the main door of her quarters creaked open. A cart rattled inside, and the food server yelled, "Dinner's by your front door, My Lord." Then the main door slammed shut. It took all of ten seconds.

From behind the closed door of Emma's bedroom, the two girls laughed.

"Thank you, Sovereign!" Chloe prayed aloud.

"Yes, indeed!" Emma added.

Leaving the bedroom, they picked up the mess the food server had made with lunch in the parlor and stacked it on the lower shelf of the food cart. Then they investigated the dumbwaiter. It still refused to operate. They tugged on the rope, but it wouldn't budge.

"I guess you're leaving through the main door," Emma said to her dubious friend, "just like a normal person."

"What about the guard?"

"Don't worry, I have a plan."

"You always do."

The pair walked to the main entrance. "By the way, the Sovereign revealed to me that your phone is still in the dumbwaiter, sitting in the downstairs kitchen. But to keep you safe, ask Junior to retrieve it."

"Got it."

"When you leave, ignore anything the guard may say and just walk away like normal, but if I tell you to run, take off as fast as you can. Though I don't think it will come to that."

"Hope not."

When Emma opened the main door of her quarters, the guard turned toward her but recoiled, shielding his eyes as if confronted by a bright light. Then he directed his attention to Chloe.

She walked past him, just as Emma had instructed.

Likely confused by Chloe's presence, the guard said nothing at first. Then he called out, "Stop!"

Chloe kept walking.

He took a step toward her. "I said stop!"

"As I see it," Emma said to the guard, "you have two choices. You can chase her and let me escape, or you can ignore her and keep me here. And if you somehow manage to do both, you'll need to explain how you let her get in in the first place."

Turning to face Emma, he crossed his arms and planted his feet right in front of the door.

Emma stood there staring at him until Chloe was safely away. Then she shut the door, debating whether she should try to study or give in to her intense desire to sleep.

14

SUSTENANCE

Instead, Emma did neither, opting to eat instead. Offering thanksgiving to the Sovereign, she cleaned out the contents of the mini fridge—save for an oatmeal roll—and downed as much water as she could. She'd been drinking all day and was peeing about, like, every hour. She imagined each trip to the bathroom washing toxins from her system—and prayed it to be so.

Emma studied for about an hour and a half, which was all she needed to do to catch up on the schoolwork she missed from Friday. Then she went to bed early, asking the Sovereign to continue to restore her body to full health.

She woke in the morning and climbed out of

bed before her alarm went off. She couldn't remember when that had last happened. The aches from her fight with the guard on Thursday night were gone. Her head was clear, and her stomach no longer cramped in protest to the poison she'd eaten. She was feeling better.

Emma decided that, as far as anyone she didn't trust would know, she was still deathly ill. She didn't need to wait long to continue her act.

She heard the food server push a cart inside her quarters. Before she could wheel away yesterday's provisions, Emma called out. "Help me!" Then she moaned as loudly as she could. "I hurt so bad. Don't let me die! Save me!"

As her bedroom doorknob turned, Emma roughed up her hair, jumped into bed, and pulled her covers up around her face. She let out the most plaintive groan she could muster.

The door opened a crack, letting in a ray of light.

"I can't stand the pain any longer," Emma wailed. "Don't let me die alone."

The door shut.

"No! Don't go! Help me! I beg you." She added a whimper for good measure.

The only response was the sound of yesterday's food cart wheeling away and the front door closing.

Emma threw back the covers with a laugh. It felt like a theater exercise, and she aced it.

But before she could get up, a voice from above echoed inside her head. *Stay in bed, Emma.*

Why? she thought back.

You'll soon have another guest . . . to entertain.

Emma lay down again. She pinched her cheeks to make them look blotchy and rubbed her eyes, hard, so it would appear she'd been crying. Then she pulled the covers tightly around her neck. Releasing the air from her lungs, she reimmersed herself in her role of a dying woman. She'd be ready when they arrived. *Who would it be?*

She didn't need to wait long. The front door to her quarters opened. Footfalls from a couple of people approached her bedroom. Without knocking, someone opened the door, but she didn't dare peek to see who it was. Instead, she groaned for effect.

"Oh, my dear little Emma." It was Pompous Jack. "I understand you're feeling unwell. I so hate to see you suffering, little one."

"Help me," she moaned.

"I can safely say that your suffering will be short. You're not likely to last the day."

Emma rolled her head to the sound of his voice, but didn't open her eyes. With a quiver, she eased her hand free of the covers and shakily rose it toward him. Then she let it fall to the bed with a thump, as though no longer strong enough to hold it up.

"The last High Priest lingered on in agony for months," Pompous Jack said, showing no emotion. "Interestingly, a miscommunication between me and your server will cut yours short. When I told her to increase the dosage two times, she thought I said ten. It's kind of ironic. Frankly, I'm surprised you've made it this long."

"Again, I apologize for my error," the food server said.

"Don't give it another thought," Pompous Jack answered.

"Thank you, Your Royal Eminence. Though I came back with you as requested, may I leave now? Being around her, even being in her quarters, frightens me to no end."

"I'm strangely uncomfortable here as well," Pompous Jack said. "I am most unsettled in her presence. You may surely leave. Rest assured I won't be far behind. See you tonight."

Emma forced her eyelids to flutter, as if she were confused and no longer in control of her body. "I hurt so bad. All over. Especially my stomach." With much drama, she curled into a fetal position, whimpering as she did. "Can you get me something for the pain?"

"Obviously, you're in no condition to take part in the Sunday service. Even so, I wasn't expecting you to be around for it, anyway. I'll explain your absence to those gathered, and you'll be long gone before next Sunday arrives. That will mark the end of Emma Barlow."

"Please!" Emma wailed to emphasize her pretend agony.

When Pompous Jack bent down and touched her face, Emma pushed back her primordial instinct to grab his finger and break it. With the adrenaline surging through her body, she sensed she could have done it. Or maybe deliver her best punch to his pious face. Instead, the Sovereign gave her strength to not react.

"That's quite a black eye you got there. No amount of makeup could ever cover it. So even if you were healthy, that alone would prevent you from taking part in today's service."

Emma wailed again, hoping she wasn't overacting. "I beg you. Please help me!"

"Why don't you just curse the Sovereign you care so deeply about and die?"

"Never!" Emma worried she said that a bit too forcefully for a person about to die.

"You should have heeded my advice and not opposed me. You should have left when you still had a chance. Instead, you forced me to carry through on my promise to put an end to your pitiful little masquerade. That means your passing will be all your fault."

Emma still wanted to punch him, but she willed herself to keep up the ruse. Instead, she breathed out as slowly as she could and gently closed her eyes. Then she held her breath. Though she'd never done a death scene before, she felt she gave a most convincing performance.

She heard Pompous Jack shuffle from the room and ease the door shut. Its latch clicked. Soon, the main door of her quarters closed as well. She threw back her covers and grabbed her cell phone. She pushed "Stop" on the voice recorder.

15

MORE MADNESS

After pretending to be dying for the last half hour, energy surged through Emma's body, now quite rested. She bounded from bed and about skipped into the kitchenette. With anticipation, she pulled open the door of the mini fridge. It was empty. Even the roll she had saved last night was gone.

That's when she remembered reading in the Holy Text about the Sovereign feeding the prophet "day by day, one cycle at a time" for over three years. He always had enough, and anything he saved for the next day always disappeared overnight.

Knowing what to do, she shut the refrigerator door, her eyes gleaming. She lifted her hands heavenward. "Thank you, Sovereign, for the food you have provided for me today—day by day. May it strengthen me and supply what I need for your honor and your kingdom. Amen."

Full of anticipation and with an expectant sparkle, Emma opened the door of the mini fridge a second time. There sat her provisions for the day—but no more.

The rest of Sunday was uneventful. Though Emma wanted to watch the Sunday service—in part to hear what Pompous Jack would say about her—she had no way to do so. Instead, she focused on getting better. She rested, ate the Sovereign's provisions, and drank as much water as her bladder would tolerate.

Her only concern was to make sure she was in bed each time the server delivered her meals, ready to reprise her role of a dying girl, in case the woman checked on her. That didn't happen, with a new food cart replacing the old, just inside the main entrance. Thankfully, the server was most punctual, arriving at 11:50 a.m. and again at 5:00 p.m.

It wasn't until 7:30 on Monday morning that the server peeked into Emma's bedroom. Emma breathed in slowly to show that she was still alive. Yet she made no other sound. She pretended she was in a coma. Though she had only seen it on TV shows before this, she felt she pulled it off well enough.

After the food server left her quarters, Emma showered and got dressed. She was running out of clean clothes to put on, but that was a minor issue, given her present situation posing as a dying woman.

After giving a faith-filled prayer of thanks for her day-by-day sustenance, she opened the mini fridge with anticipation to see what delicious food the Sovereign had provided.

The Almighty did not disappoint.

After breakfast, she waited in the study, but her tutor never showed. This delighted Emma. She did her schoolwork on her own, finishing for the day by 10:30. That's when she heard men's muffled voices arguing outside the door to her quarters.

Your father's here to see you, whispered the Sovereign in Emma's spirit. *Make sure the guard doesn't send him away again.*

Emma strode to the door, wondering what role she would need to play. Obviously, she couldn't be a bedridden coma patient. Yet she couldn't behave how she felt either, which was nearly normal. So she ruffled her hair, pinched her cheeks a couple times, and hunched her shoulders forward. She squinted her eyes and opened the door with a shuffle.

There stood her dad, squared off in a face-to-face confrontation with the guard. Her presence surprised both, her dad emoting concern and the guard in wide-eyed shock.

"I was informed you were in a coma," the guard said.

"Thank you for sending for my doctor," Emma croaked in a husky whisper. Moving as if she were an invalid, she eased the door to her quarters open.

Her father stepped forward, but the guard held up his hand. "I wasn't aware you were her doctor or informed you were summoned," he said to Emma's dad. "I must search you before I let you in."

The guard took her father's cell phone, along with a second one in his medical bag. "You can have them back when you leave." After a thorough search, he approved the rest of the bag's contents, saying, "It sure looks like medical stuff to me."

Emma's dad rushed into her quarters and pulled the door shut. Only then did she roll back her shoulders, hold her head high, and smile.

"I've been trying to get to you ever since His Royal Eminence announced you were refusing to eat and slipping into a coma."

"No worries, Dad. I was just acting."

He looked at her, glanced at the cart of uneaten food, and back to her. "I don't understand. You're okay?"

"They've been poisoning my food and water, but once I realized it, I stopped eating it. I think it's mostly out of my system now."

He already had his penlight out and was peering into her pupils, checking for responsiveness. "Your black eye concerns me. How badly does it hurt?

"It's fine. The Sovereign healed me."

To Emma's surprise, her father accepted her answer. "How long have you gone without food?"

"The Sovereign's been feeding me day by day, and the water in the shower is safe to drink."

He grabbed her wrist to check her pulse. "How do you know the food was poisoned?"

"The Sovereign revealed it to me, and I confirmed it by looking at it with my spirit."

He pulled out his stethoscope.

"Dad, before you have a heart attack, take a deep breath. I'm okay. Let's sit down and talk." Emma led him into the living room, where she plopped on the couch.

He sat next to her and pulled out a blood pressure cuff.

"If I let you go through all your tests and stuff, will you stop freaking out?"

"I'll answer that once I complete my preliminary examination."

Emma patiently let him.

At last, he admitted she appeared to be physically fine. "Let me do a blood draw for analysis and investigate the supposed poisoning."

"There's nothing supposed about it. I was poisoned. I almost died. But the Sovereign protected me . . . and healed me."

"I'll also take a sample of the food and water for testing."

"Maybe then you'll believe me."

"What's been happening? Your mother and I have been quite concerned, especially after your phone stopped working. You've not responded to emails, and as of Friday, Chloe and Joshua hadn't heard from you either.

"Don't overreact—because I'm okay, remember?

"Here's an overview. I've been locked in my quarters since Thursday and had no contact with anyone except my tutor and food server—who's been poisoning me. My tutor is cruel, and she took my laptop. He somehow turned off my phone. Oh, and he also took my copy of the Holy Text and my journal of notes."

"He? You mean His Royal Eminence?"

"Exactly! I told you he wasn't to be trusted. Remember?"

"I'm starting to realize that."

"Let's see. What else? I contacted Gabe in the spiritual realm, and he sent Junior to help. Junior gave me some food and then went out to get me a prepaid phone. Chloe came up and spent Friday evening and all day Saturday with me."

"Junior did indeed buy you a phone, but he couldn't deliver it. I had it in my bag, but the guard took it." Her dad cocked his head in confusion. "How did Chloe get into your quarters with an armed guard out front?"

"There's a dumbwaiter between my quarters and the kitchen below. We used it for a while, but it stopped working."

"You mean Chloe got in through a dumbwaiter?"

"It was a tight fit, but that's what she did. I tried to use it to escape, but I'm too tall, along with being claustrophobic and all. I think that brings you up to date."

"Wait!" her dad interjected. "Chloe saw you on Saturday? I wonder why she didn't update us?"

"She lost her phone."

Her dad scrunched up his face. "Surely she had other options." He shook his head. "Emma, we had no idea what you were going through."

She shifted on the couch and rotated so she could better look at her dad. "My turn now. With Mondays being your busiest day of the week, how come you're here and not working?"

"You're more important."

"What aren't you telling me?"

"It's nothing. Don't worry."

"Spill." Emma stared at her father and didn't blink.

He eventually gave in to her piercing glare. "I have the day off."

"You never get a day off. What's the real story?"

Her dad looked away and gulped. "I don't want you to worry, but they fired me." Then his eyes brightened a bit. "I guess that means I now have a lot of days off."

Her father's situation angered her, but she

wasn't surprised. "It was because of me, wasn't it?" She waited for him to verify what she already knew.

He gave her a somber downward tip of his head.

"If you no longer have a job, how will you get my blood analyzed and the food tested?"

"I'll figure something out."

"Contact Captain Hernandez. I'm sure he can make it happen. Joshua has his number."

"That's a brilliant suggestion."

Emma wondered how long her dad would be unemployed. He was an excellent doctor, and, given the shortage of healthcare workers, she assumed it wouldn't be long. Then she realized he might need to move. That concerned her even more. It was hard enough being in the High Priest's residence in the Temple Palace and not home with her family, but at least they were in the same city. Yet if they had to move, the chance to see them each week would leave with them.

Then another worry hit her. "What about Mom? Does she still have her job?"

"Her company laid her off too."

"The sibs? Please tell me they're all right."

"Aside from some typical middle school drama last Wednesday, Hailey and Brayden are fine. Even so, we kept them out of school the last two days, just to be safe."

"I'm so sorry." Pompous Jack had a bigger reach and more influence than she'd ever imagined. "I never meant for any of this to hurt you."

He reached out to hold her hand. The warmth of his touch brought comfort. "Don't worry about us. The main thing right now is to get you out of here and keep you safe."

"I'm working on some ideas. I trust the Sovereign will show me what to do when the time comes—just like always."

16

___

GUARD BE GONE

fter her father left, Emma spent some time worshiping and praying. She listened to the Sovereign for direction.

The man who assaulted you is guarding your front door, the Sovereign revealed to Emma.

Emma believed the Sovereign's words, but she needed ideas on what to do. She opened the door a few inches to check things out.

The guard turned toward her but pulled away as he covered his face, just like the first guard had done when Chloe had left Saturday evening, and the other guard did a few hours earlier. Recovering from his shock, he sneered at her. "I wish you'd just die."

His matter-of-fact demeanor irritated Emma.

"I should have ended you last week when I had the chance."

"But I'm still here, and you're still stuck guarding me." In a way, he was a prisoner too.

"I'm impressed with your black eye. My only regret is not giving you two."

"My black eye will go away, but the four scratches I gave you will last a long time." Not wanting to banter anymore, Emma shut the door. She knew what she needed to know. He was alone and stationed as usual.

Summon the police, the Sovereign prompted Emma in her spirit.

I can't. My phone doesn't work, remember?

You can still use it to make an emergency call.

Emma had forgotten that. She imagined what she'd say. Though it would require little acting, she prepared herself for this new role.

Taking a fresh breath, she dialed 911.

"Nine-one-one. What is your emergency?"

"This is Emma Barlow. I'm in the High Priest's residence at the Temple Palace. The man who assaulted me last week is back and threatening me again." Having given the key facts, she now needed to sell it. "He's holding me prisoner. I'm afraid he's going to kill me."

"Please stay on the line, My Lord, while I summon help. Don't hang up."

"I won't. Please hurry." Emma hoped that last line didn't sound too desperate. In truth, with the Sovereign's protection, she wasn't afraid at all. She was just irritated with the situation, especially with Pompous Jack.

Within seconds, the emergency dispatcher returned to the line. "Two squad cars are on the way. I've also alerted Captain Hernandez, who's heading out as well, even as we speak."

"Thank you. I feel better already."

"I'm happy to serve you, My Lord."

Emma resisted the urge to encourage the dispatcher to call her Emma instead of My Lord. "What's your name?"

"I am but a humble servant."

"What do your family and friends call you?"

The dispatcher hesitated and finally spoke. "Martha."

"Well, Martha, thank you for helping me!"

Though Martha remained guarded in what she said, the two of them had a meaningful conversation as Emma encouraged her on her faith journey. Only when Emma heard the officers outside and Martha confirmed they were there did they end their call.

Emma opened the door to her residence. There stood two officers flanking the guard. Again, he recoiled at her presence, but the two officers did not. If anything, they seemed drawn to her. As Captain Hernandez strode toward them, Emma stretched out her arm and aimed a defiant finger at the guard. "That's the man who assaulted me last week. He's the one who did this!" She pointed to her black eye with both index fingers.

"Arrest him!" Hernandez bellowed.

"It wasn't me!" the man protested. "You have no evidence. It's her word against mine. I demand you arrest her for slander."

Emma raised the palm of her right hand before her and curled her fingers to study them. "What about your DNA under my fingernails from when I clawed you?" Then she held up her hand, palm out, toward the man's four scars on his cheek. "Should we see how well my fingers align?"

There was no need. The officers had already handcuffed the guard and started dragging him away. That's when he turned around. "Yes, I did it! But I'm not taking the fall alone. His Royal Eminence was behind it. Arrest him too."

Once he was safely away, the captain turned to

Emma. "With you identifying him as your attacker and his confession, we can safely close this case. But we don't have DNA evidence, and any traces under your fingernails are long gone."

"We know that, but he didn't."

The corner of Captain Hernandez's mouth twitched. "Nicely played."

Emma opened the door for him, and he walked in. She guided him to the study, figuring it was the best place for them to meet.

She updated him on what had happened to her the last several days, and he apologized for not being able to respond quicker. "But know," he said, "I've given this my full attention and had teams working on it around the clock. Your call was the break we needed, and his confession will seal his conviction."

When the captain heard about her non-working phone, he shook his head. "That should have never happened." Then he made a call with his, communicated the details, and gave the simple instruction, "Take care of it."

"Thank you," Emma said. "I feel lost without it."

As they chatted, he gawked at her face. His

focused attention on her black eye made her squirm.

When the captain noticed Emma's discomfort, he explained. "Forgive me for staring, but the black and blue bruises around your eye are fading. I've watched them go from black, to dark gray, to light gray. At this rate it should be back to normal within seconds."

Now everything made sense to Emma. "Last week I asked the Sovereign to restore it, but nothing happened until right now. I guess I needed it to look bad until after you arrested the guard."

"I've never witnessed such a thing." Hernandez shook his head. "But if you're involved, I should now know to expect the unexpected."

He rose to leave. That's when Emma made her request. "Have you checked the palace security cams?"

He looked at her quizzically. "The video is erased every twenty-four hours as it records new footage. What we could access gave little information."

"You need to go back further," Emma said. "I sense the files are backed up before being overwritten, but I don't know anything more."

"Interesting. I certainly trust your insight, vague

as it is. Once we locate these files, what should we look for?"

Emma didn't know, but then an idea came to her supernaturally. "Look into the people who arrive and how long they stay. Figure out who they are and determine their age."

"What will that reveal to us?"

"The answers you seek." Emma didn't mean to be evasive, but that was all she knew.

Captain Hernandez seemed to accept this. "We'll get on it right away."

When the pair reached the main door to the residence, there stood a new guard in front of the door. Like his predecessors, he pulled back and shielded his eyes when he saw Emma.

"What is the meaning of this?" Hernandez barked.

"I'm here to protect the High Priestess."

"No!" Emma crossed her arms. "You're here to make sure I can't leave."

"You're free to go anywhere you want," the guard said, "and I will accompany you to ensure your safety here on the Temple grounds."

The captain considered his pledge. "If the High Priestess ever tells me otherwise, we'll arrest you too."

After thanking Captain Hernandez for all he had done, Emma decided to test the guard's claim. "I'm going for lunch." She headed to the cafeteria. To her surprise, the guard allowed her to leave and fell in step behind her.

"You're not here to keep me safe, are you? You're here to make sure I don't do anything to tick off your boss."

He didn't reply; she hadn't expected him to.

About halfway to the cafeteria, they met Jennifer pushing a food cart toward the Temple Palace. Squealing with delight, Emma ran up to her and wrapped her arms around her friend.

"I was thinking about eating in the cafeteria today."

"Since I already have our meals prepared, let's head back to your place."

Emma agreed. "I'm so glad you're back. I didn't like that other food server—not at all."

"The police arrested her this morning for trying to poison you. I doubt we'll ever see her again."

Emma and Jennifer strolled to the palace, with her guard trailing behind. Knowing there'd be plenty of food, Emma invited him in for lunch. Though she didn't want him to join them, it was the right thing to do. She wanted to show him the

Sovereign's unmerited love, even if he didn't deserve it.

He shook his head and took a step back. "I appreciate the offer, but please don't insist I come inside. The place freaks me out."

Remembering her prayer to consecrate her residence, Emma accepted his answer and left him standing guard at the door.

As they set the table for lunch, Emma's phone vibrated. It was a message from Captain Hernandez. "Your phone is again working, with safeguards to keep anyone from deactivating it in the future."

"Thank you!!!!!" she texted back.

As the pair enjoyed lunch, they filled each other in on the last couple of days. They had a lot of catching up to do. Being with Jennifer filled her with joy. Even better would be for her to see Joshua, gaze into his beautiful brown eyes, and feel her heart go pitter-patter.

A knock on the dining room door interrupted her bliss. It was her tutor. "I was pleased to hear about your recovery and came right away to resume your studies."

Emma hid her frustration. "I appreciate that, but there's no need. I've decided to be homeschooled instead and don't need a tutor. I'll text Principal Johnson after lunch." Then Emma tipped her head toward the tote bag slung over the tutor's shoulder. "Can I have my laptop?"

Emma could see the tutor struggling to corral her thoughts as she returned the computer. "I could oversee your homeschooling and relieve your parents of that responsibility. I understand they're going through quite a bit right now."

"Thank you, but no need." Emma reached out to lay her hand on Jennifer's. "Jennifer is a certified teacher and will oversee my homeschooling."

17

A HEAVENLY TRIP

"Homeschool?" Jennifer beamed at Emma. Delight shone on her face, but confusion soon replaced it. "Obviously, I'd love to. But I already have too much to do."

"I've been thinking about that," Emma said. "If I ate all my meals in the cafeteria, wouldn't that free up most of your time?"

"I suppose so. I'd need to check with my supervisor."

"Isn't your mother your supervisor? I'm sure she'd approve."

"I'm sure she would, too, especially coming from you." Jennifer looked to her left for a few seconds before returning her gaze. "But I worry it could have a negative impact on the whole department. It would just seem like more work for them to do—and they already have too much."

"I'm working on some ideas for that too."

Jennifer stopped eating to consider Emma's surprising statement. "Aside from the impact on the Temple staff, I think me homeschooling you could work, but you'd need to do some subjects online . . . like art and computer science, the ones I'm weak in. I suspect there'd be extra paperwork to fill out for me to serve as your parents' proxy."

"Great! I'll text Principal Johnson, and then we can talk to your mother."

"Let's put that second part on hold. I'll talk to her first. The thought of being in your presence makes her squirm."

The pair agreed on how to proceed. Jennifer returned to the cafeteria to talk to her mom, and Emma got her parents' blessing to have Jennifer oversee her homeschooling. Next, she contacted Principal Johnson. By the time she met Jennifer at the cafeteria for dinner, Emma had completed all the paperwork and only needed her instructor's signature. They could start tomorrow.

Emma wrapped up the day connecting with Joshua. What started as a long text string morphed into an even longer video call, lasting over two hours. It felt so good to spend time with him.

Emma settled into bed. She thanked the Sovereign for her freedom, a plan for homeschooling, and her future with Joshua. Only her escalating conflict with Pompous Jack remained.

Emma closed her eyes and prayed. She felt the Divine Spirit within her grow stronger. Warmth flowed through her body. Peace flooded her soul. She lifted both arms heavenward and recited the passage of the Holy Text that Gabe had shared with her, the words that had begun her journey to becoming the new High Priest.

"Approach the Sovereign with a pure heart and live; those with selfish intent will perish—be it in body or in spirit." Whether she said this aloud or in her spirit, she wasn't sure. It didn't matter. The Sovereign would receive it just the same.

"Approach the Sovereign with a pure heart," she repeated. "Approach the Sovereign with a pure heart. Approach the Sovereign with a pure heart."

That's when she felt her spirit slide out of her body's protective shell. The two parts separated with ease, peacefully. Excitement surged in her soul as her spirit ascended, leaving behind the concerns of earth, along with her physical covering.

Though she no longer had a body with arms and legs, face and hair, and mouth and eyes, they continued to provide sensations as if they still existed. Faster and faster she rose, blowing her ethereal hair back. The rapid ascent stirred her spirit. She would soon be in the Sovereign's presence. That's what mattered. That's *all* that mattered.

Below her, the bed in her quarters, and even the palace, shrunk into a tiny dot and then disappeared. The earth dimmed, light gray at first and then growing darker, as she neared the intense glow radiating from the Sovereign in heaven.

The white aura of her spirit approached the even brighter brilliance of the Sovereign. Emma sensed her hands—even though they didn't exist in the supernatural realm—reach to hug the Almighty. Unexplainable joy surged through her being. There was no better place to be than to sit in the Sovereign's presence.

The Sovereign embraced Emma.

She could stay in this moment forever. She knew that for sure.

Soon the Sovereign's thoughts entered Emma's spirit. *I know you have a question for me, but realize that you can inquire of me any time you want. You don't need to be in my presence to seek my input.*

This disappointed Emma. She'd been waiting for several days to ask the Sovereign in person—face-to-face, if you will—but she could have asked it right away. She'd do that as soon as she returned to earth.

But since you're here, the Sovereign added, *I'll answer your query. Yes, the auditorium—and the Temple before it—are extravagant displays of adoration toward me. It honors me. To be frank—without a hint of arrogance—nothing is too excessive when it comes to worshiping me. I would have, however, preferred the money be used to advance my kingdom and help those in need.*

How can we best do that? In her spirit, Emma tucked a strand of hair behind her ear, even though none of that was physically present.

My followers advance my kingdom when they help the poor, heal the sick, and point people to me.

Please help me do that when I return.

Know that I will, came the Sovereign's words. *But first you must rest in my presence. You have undergone much, and it will take time for your spirit to recover. That is why I allowed you to approach my heavenly throne.*

Though Emma had focused on her body's healing, she didn't realize her spirit might need rest too. She opened herself to receive all the restoration the Almighty would give.

You will soon face two mighty battles, one interdimensional and the other strictly spiritual. The first will test you, and the second will temper you. Both involve that evil man you call Pompous Jack.

Emma grew somber. *Is he the devil incarnate?*

Technically, no, but from your perspective, that may be the best way to understand his threat.

When we do battle, will I be fighting the devil himself? The thought concerned Emma, and she needed to know.

In essence you will, but know that I will be with you. I am always with you.

Why can't you just fight the devil yourself and leave me out of it?

Many battles occur between my followers and his, the Sovereign responded. *Though I am omnipotent and have the power to fight each one myself, that would not allow my children to become stronger.*

Emma's spirit took in all that the Sovereign gave her, growing brighter and stronger as she did. Whether this took seconds or hours, she wasn't sure. Since the Sovereign existed outside of time, it didn't matter.

Arise my child. Return to your earthly home and face your first battle.

18

THE TEST

Emma's spirit eased away from the Sovereign. She knew this would happen, but leaving her supernatural bliss made her sad. Her return to earth picked up speed just as before. Yet as she left the heavenly realm behind her and the earth grew larger, her descent slowed. Something was wrong.

The Temple Palace came into view. She focused on her quarters and then her bed. That's when she saw it. More correctly, that's when she didn't see it. Her body wasn't there.

Her spirit seemed intent on returning to the exact spot where it had left her body. Yet if her body wasn't there, how could they reunite?

Her descent stopped and then reversed. She

ascended toward heaven, but the Sovereign prevented her from returning, giving a simple instruction: *Search for your body.*

Then her spirit moved back toward earth, but as she got closer, it recoiled and went up again. Like a yo-yo, her spirit bounced back and forth between heaven and earth, alternately approaching both but reaching neither.

She must discover where her body was if she had any hope for her spirit to merge back into it. Emma lost track of how many times she bobbed back and forth between heaven and earth. Though she knew how to seek someone's spirit, she wasn't sure if that would work for a body, especially when it was her own.

At the top of her upward path, she spun her spirit to scan every direction. She zeroed in on the hospital and sensed her body was there. She steered her spirit to it, but each time she veered a few yards from her fixed course, it snapped her back like a taut rubber band, as if intent on sending her spirit to her bed and nowhere else.

Peering into the hospital, she spotted what she sought. In a room on the sixth floor, her body lay unmoving on the bed. Her father sat in the chair next to it, holding her hand. Her mother sat on the other side, stroking her other hand.

Medical monitors flanked the bed, with flashing displays and rhythmic beeps. She heard her parents talking.

"I suppose we should be grateful His Royal Eminence discovered her in a coma-like state and had her transported to the hospital," her father said.

"But with him involved, I'm worried." Her mother caressed Emma's cheek. "Quite worried."

"We have every reason to be." Her father bent down and kissed her hand.

Emma tried to reach out to him. She connected with his spirit. *Dad, can you hear me?*

He lifted his head and scooted closer to her bed. "Emma, did you say something?" He looked at Emma's mom. "Did you hear anything?"

She shook her head.

That's when Emma reached out to her mother's spirit and connected. "Mom, this is Emma. Can you hear me? I'm contacting you from the spiritual realm."

"Yes!" her mother said with excitement. "I did hear something. She just called me."

"That's strange," her dad said. "I didn't hear

her call you, but a few seconds ago, I heard her call me."

Emma tried several more times to reach them but failed. In the end, they concluded they were under too much stress and just imagining things. After that she couldn't even connect with their spirits.

That's when she tried Joshua. She found him in the waiting room outside and connected with him right away. *Joshua, can you hear me?*

He perked up and looked around.

Joshua! I'm trying to reach you from the spiritual realm.

He closed his eyes and opened his spirit to connect with hers. *Yes, I hear you! What in the world is happening?*

My spirit ascended to heaven to hang out with the Sovereign, but when I returned to earth, my body wasn't where I left it. You need to get it back there so my spirit can rejoin it.

I'm on it! Joshua dashed into her hospital room, surprising both of her parents. "Emma's spirit just reached out to mine. She's not in a coma. We need to get her body back to her bedroom at the palace so her spirit can rejoin it. Then she'll be okay."

Her parents shared a quizzical glance and then

nodded in unison, confirming they'd help Joshua with his strange request.

Her dad knew just what to do. "Once I disconnect the monitors, we'll need to move fast before the nurse comes in to check. For once, the hospital being short-staffed will work in our favor."

"I'll get the car and wait for you out back," her mom said.

Joshua followed her out of Emma's room and searched for a wheelchair. It didn't take long. When he returned, Emma's dad explained the steps they would take and the precise order they would do them.

Keeping her connected to the main monitors, her dad and Joshua shifted her body into the wheelchair. Emma's dad disconnected the remaining devices as fast as he could. They left the room in haste, but not so fast as to attract attention. They had almost made it to the elevator when a nurse called out and chased them down the hall. The doors opened, and they wheeled Emma inside.

"Go!" Joshua said. "I'll run interference." Holding up his arms, he blocked the nurse before she could stop them.

The elevator doors eased shut. She glared at him.

"Don't worry." Joshua dropped his arms to his sides. "He's a doctor. Everything will be okay."

Though Emma wanted to keep watching Joshua, she was more interested in her body's escape. She tried again to reach her father in her spirit. Though she still couldn't communicate, his spirit was open enough for her to connect with him and see what he was seeing. The elevator opened, and he pushed her wheelchair outside to her mom in the waiting car.

Hurry! Emma called out in her spirit.

Her dad jostled her into the car and fell in awkwardly behind her. "Go!" He jerked the door shut.

Her mother squealed the car forward as a security guard ran out of the hospital, waving his arms and screaming, "Stop!"

They didn't.

Her mom drove like a maniac for a couple of blocks and then slowed down, taking deep breaths as if to push the adrenaline from her body. Now safely away, she drove the speed limit and obeyed every traffic sign.

Though Emma wanted her body back in her room as fast as possible, she didn't want to risk hurting anyone else. That's when she focused on slowing her spiritual pulse.

As her mother drove, her father attended to her in the back seat. He shifted her body to a less awkward position and buckled her in. He did the same for himself. Once secure, he checked her pulse. Satisfied with the results, he examined her eyes, timed her breathing, and felt her forehead for a fever, which was all he could do without medical equipment.

"She's in stable condition," he said. "I sure hope Joshua knew what he was talking about, and this will all work out."

Her parents remained quiet the rest of the way.

As they drove, Emma's spirit kept bobbing up and down between heaven and earth, with each trip taking her closer to the palace and further from the Sovereign's supernatural home.

When they pulled up to the Temple Palace, Emma's downward trip brought her close to the roof. In her spirit, she stretched out her arms to grab the top, but she bounced up and pulled away.

Her parents got out of the car and several priests from Gamma group rushed up, carrying a stretcher. With care—much more so than when they placed her in the car—her parents moved her body and placed it on the stretcher. Four priests carried it, with the others surrounding her for protection.

By the time they reached the door to her residence, Emma's up and down bobbing took her as low as the ceiling to her bedroom. If they moved quickly, her next downward descent may let her spirit reconnect with her body. *Hurry*, she called out in her spirit, just in case any of them could hear her from the spiritual realm.

"Leave her on the stretcher and just lay it in the middle of the bed," her father said.

They did. Her body was close to where it was when her spirit left. Yet it wasn't in the exact spot.

Is it close enough? Emma wondered. Soon she would find out.

This time her spirit dropped even lower, past the ceiling and toward her body. The disconnected parts of her essence reunited and interlocked, much like a seat belt clicking in place when buckled.

Emma's chest expanded mightily as her lungs filled with air. Her eyes popped open, and she sat up.

"Hi!"

19

———

REUNION

Emma scanned the room full of people surrounding her bed. For the first time, the situation didn't make her squirm. "Thank you!" Gratitude beamed from her face. "I really appreciate all you did. I wasn't sure if I'd make it, but thanks to you all, everything worked out."

Without a word, the priests shuffled out, in order from youngest to oldest. That left Emma with her parents. "You two were especially amazing! I saw everything you did."

"Joshua helped too," her dad added. "He stayed back to ensure we could get away. He was brilliant. Too bad he's not here to celebrate."

Emma reached out in her spirit to locate Joshua.

"He's on his way right now, along with Chloe and Junior. Topher's driving."

Emma's parents exchanged questioning glances, something that now occurred often with Emma's growing understanding of the supernatural.

"He'll be here in five."

As they waited for Joshua to arrive, Emma's dad returned to doctor mode and assessed her condition —again. In a few minutes, he announced his conclusion. "Everything I can check looks great." He straightened his frame, switching from doctor back to Dad.

That's when Joshua ran in and gave Emma a ginormous hug. She wanted a kiss, too, but hoped he would wait. Not in front of her parents. Not yet.

Chloe and Junior followed, with Topher trailing behind.

"Figures we'd miss all the excitement," Chloe said. "We picked the wrong time to take a lunch break, but when we got to your room and heard you'd escaped, we headed here right away." She reached out to touch Emma. Her eyes grew misty, and her voice quivered. "We were so worried and said a lot of prayers."

It wasn't long before Jennifer rushed in. Her

ashen face brightened when she saw that Emma was okay.

Next came Ashley. She nestled in next to Topher, and their fingers interlocked. Emma's eyes connected with Ashley's, and she flashed a quick wink of approval to her new friend.

That's when Emma noticed Gabe standing in the corner. *How long had he been there?* He gave her an approving nod, leaving Emma to wonder how much he knew about her ordeal.

She surveyed the group. Two weeks ago, she didn't even know half of them, but they were her people now. The ones she knew she could depend on whatever the situation. Aside from the sibs, everyone she cared about was in the room at this moment. Emotion overtook her, and tears of joy flowed.

That's when Emma's stomach rumbled, loudly. No one said a thing, but a snicker snuck out of Chloe's mouth, and soon everyone was laughing.

"Who wants lunch?" Emma surveyed the group. They all seemed receptive.

Jennifer tipped her head toward the cafeteria, confirming what Emma was thinking.

"Let's head to the cafeteria to celebrate."

20

THE DUEL

Throughout lunch, Emma wondered when Pompous Jack would show up and ruin all their fun, but he never did. Searching for him in her spirit, Emma confirmed he wasn't on the Temple grounds. He seemed far away. She sensed he might be meeting with the Prime Minister, but she wasn't sure why she thought that. Was it a supernatural revelation?

Emma returned from lunch to discover one of Pompous Jack's guards again stationed at the door to her residence. As she drew close, his body shuddered, and he averted his eyes.

"I relieve you of your position," Emma said. "Please give Junior your keys and equipment."

When the guard objected, she hinted that he could be arrested if he stuck around—for being complicit in the attack on her. He scurried off. After supper, she also fired Pompous Jack's two remaining guards. They left without complaint.

This meant she had only Pompous Jack to deal with before she could move forward with her planned reforms. She sensed their confrontation would happen soon.

Emma went to bed early, but not to sleep. She wanted to pray and worship first. By midnight her spirit was filled with contentment, and her soul overflowed with peace. She felt ready. She wasn't placing her confidence in her own ability, however, but in the Almighty's power and protection. Closing her eyes, she fell asleep within seconds.

In the middle of the night, something crashed. Panic surged through her like a bolt of lightning. Her spirit went on high alert, searching for what caused the noise. She knew she was safe in her consecrated quarters, but a storm brewed about.

Trembling, she moved into the supernatural realm. Her glowing spirit entered an inky darkness that surrounded her new home. Evil lurked. She moved into it, shining brightly, making her an easy target. A supernatural duel with Pompous Jack awaited. Demons swirled around. They noticed her right away and shrieked. In her spirit, she moved her ethereal arm from left to right, giving a dismissive flick with the back of her hand. The evil spirits recoiled in horror and fluttered away, leaving only a foreboding void. She did this without thinking, and their response surprised her, even as she scolded herself for doubting.

It wasn't long before the spirit of Pompous Jack arrived. His darkness filled the space. Though the Sovereign had said he wasn't technically the devil incarnate, it sure felt that way to Emma. She pushed her terror aside. Once this would have petrified her, but not anymore. The Sovereign had taught her. The Sovereign had strengthened her. And the Sovereign had prepared her for this very moment.

Having the Divine Spirit within her filled her with confidence. She was on the winning side and Pompous Jack would lose. She had faith she would succeed, yet she knew she would need to first prevail in an epic supernatural battle, one far beyond any fight she'd ever encountered.

With an unearthly snarl, Pompous Jack's spirit lunged toward hers. She moved aside and deftly dodged his charge. Yet when she turned around, he was already making his second run. This time, she couldn't avoid his attack. This time their spirits collided, with them bouncing apart like sparring sumo wrestlers. Stunned, he floated aimlessly, unmoored and out of control, but so was she.

Still dazed, she pulled back an unearthly arm and launched an attack toward him. It shot forth as a bolt of light, hitting him squarely with a thud. Grunting, he disappeared, while her white aura grew.

She wondered how she had shot forth the light and if she could do it again. She also strained to discover other tools she could muster to fight her enemy.

Help me, Sovereign, she begged.

Trust me, came a quick answer.

When Pompous Jack reappeared, he launched his next attack by throwing a ball of black her way. She didn't react fast enough, and the single projectile grazed her side, splintering off shards of white. A supernatural sting shot through her being. Shocked, it was the first time she had ever felt pain when in the spiritual realm. Now knowing how vulnerable she was confirmed how much was at stake.

Bolstered in part by the throbbing, but mostly

through irritation, a righteous energy surged within. She launched a rapid-fire torrent toward her nemesis.

Though he barely avoided the first shaft of light, the rest hit their mark, but with different degrees of accuracy. Each one, however, shot out with more power than the one before it. The final one cracked forth like a bolt of lightning, hitting him squarely. He screeched in pain. As his essence again vanished, he lobbed a projectile in her direction.

I must protect myself. Emma's thought emerged as a plea to the Sovereign.

Use your shield, came the reply.

This irritated Emma. *I have no shield.*

Just believe. Receive it in faith.

As Emma did, a supernatural protection appeared before her. It was a shield, a faith shield. Large enough to cover her essence, she could move the heavy object with ease. She shifted it right and then left, up and then down, testing its maneuverability.

As the slow-moving ball of black inched toward her, she positioned her faith shield to block its flight. The projectile made contact, but she felt only a slight vibration. The shell shattered into hundreds of splinters, which harmlessly skittered away. A white light coming from her being surged out in all directions.

Emma now had a faith shield to protect her and could shoot lightning bolts to attack him. Next time, she would try to throw projectiles too. This would give her assault a one-two punch, just like a boxer striving to take down an opponent.

What else can I do? Emma asked the Sovereign.

Call forth Scripture. Evil recoils when my people recite the Holy Text.

Emma knew just what to say. She'd be ready when Pompous Jack returned, which she sensed could be at any moment. Though she wished she'd been more committed about memorizing Scripture, she already recalled several passages to use.

As Pompous Jack returned, this time his reemergence dawdled, as if injured. She hoped so. As for herself, she felt stronger. Her white aura beamed with power.

He first appeared as a small gray dot, which took several seconds to grow into his being's full size. As he enlarged, his image became darker but stopped short of the glossy black she knew too well as revealing his true nature.

She hesitated. Was it wrong to attack an enemy

when they were down? Though she wanted to defeat him—she must defeat him—she wanted to win with honor. Her success must come without disgrace. Yet she also realized he would not give her the same courtesy.

That's when he launched his next barrage. It popped forth like slow-moving shot from an old BB gun. Though she probably didn't need her faith shield to protect her this time, she held it up just in case.

As she waited for the pellets to arrive, she called out, "Approach the Sovereign with a pure heart and live; those with selfish intent will perish—be it in body or in soul."

The words from the Holy Text assaulted his spirit. He trembled.

"Those with selfish intent will perish—be it in body or in soul." She called this out with more confidence.

His being in the spiritual realm shook as he squirmed at the impact of the holy words. His spirit shriveled, and his darkness dimmed.

"Those with selfish intent will perish!" She yelled it with conviction.

He shivered and shimmied and shrunk.

"The Sovereign demands justice," she called

out. "The unjust will perish along with their folly." Emma's light shone brighter.

Quaking, his darkness faded to gray.

That's when she gave him her one-two punch. From her left shot a bolt of lightning headed toward the center of his being. Though she didn't know how she did it, from her right sped a missile to pummel him once her blast of light left him dazed and vulnerable.

"In his lust for power," she proclaimed, "he yielded to temptation and gave his soul to the devil." Her words arrived just after the bolt of light and just before the projectile hit him.

All hit their mark. All accomplished their goal. What remained of him shrank into a tiny, ashen dot and popped into oblivion. She didn't know if this meant he was dead or merely that his spirit sustained a life-threatening wound.

More light emanated from her being and filled the space. Demons, who had watched the battle from afar, scurried away. As they fled, they murmured their horror over the defeat of one so powerful.

Their departure revealed an array of angels positioned behind them. They celebrated Emma's victory with shouts of jubilation. That's when she realized they'd been cheering for her the entire time as they prayed for her success.

With the Sovereign by her side, she had indeed triumphed in her duel with the devil. Her fight was over—at least for now.

21

THE END

Emma rolled over with a most plaintive moan rasping from her parched lips. Her body ached. Every muscle throbbed. Every joint shot painful reminders surging through her frame.

Light leaked in through the bedroom's weighty window treatments. She had to get up, but she certainly didn't want to. This wasn't her normal reluctance to embrace a new day. It was more severe, much more.

Her spirit begged the Sovereign for strength. *Help me, please!* With a groan, Emma lifted her arms upward to receive the Sovereign's blessing. Supernatural power flowed into her. She absorbed all that the Sovereign sent, every drop. Patiently taking it all in, she now had within her what she needed.

Moving slowly, she arose from her bed and turned on the light. Her left shoulder and bicep throbbed worse than the rest of her body. Bright red scrapes adorned her upper arm. Her shoulder boasted black and blue hues, which she suspected would grow more vibrant as the day went on.

She brought her hand to the center of the pain and was about to ask the Sovereign for healing when she thought better of it. Perhaps she should leave it to remind her of the night's ordeal, of her victory . . . and of her vulnerability. She sensed the Sovereign's pleasure over her decision.

With care, she readied herself for the day. As she did, she looked forward to enjoying a hearty breakfast with Jennifer in the parlor. That's when she remembered today was to be her first breakfast in the cafeteria. This was to free up Jennifer to oversee her schooling.

Of all the days since she'd been here, this was the one time when she wanted someone to serve her a meal. *Why did we have to start today?*

After breakfast, she and Jennifer returned to the

study for her first day of homeschool at the palace. She had trouble focusing, but the morning was more to pave the way to begin her studies in earnest tomorrow. She was glad for a one-day reprieve.

Topher had left this morning to pick up His Royal Eminence from his meeting with the Prime Minister at the capital. The trip would take about six hours, but he pledged to keep Emma updated with their progress so she could be ready for Pompous Jack's return. Though she still had no idea what to do when she saw him, she trusted the Sovereign would reveal the next step when the time came.

As she prayed and prepared herself for whatever might occur, Captain Hernandez arrived. He had news, but the wounds on her shoulder and arm distracted him. "What happened?"

Emma considered her words. "It's hard to explain in a way that doesn't seem crazy, but last night I had a battle in the spiritual realm with evil. I guess these are my battle scars."

"Against His Royal Eminence?" the captain asked.

"Yes, but I suspect he's in worse shape than me."

"Speaking of His Royal Eminence, we have

enough evidence to arrest him when he returns." The captain glanced at his watch. "Which should be in about ten minutes."

The pair waited for Topher's text of their arrival. Once they received confirmation of Pompous Jack's return, Emma went first; Captain Hernandez would follow later.

She headed to Pompous Jack's office. She wanted to see him before his arrest. Sitting at his desk, his visage shocked her. Though wearing his normal designer pinstripe suit, he no longer carried it with dignity. His shoulders sagged, and his head drooped. Sunken eyes, surrounded by a bruised face, looked up at her. He no longer seemed to be someone to fear, but as someone to pity.

Yet she knew better. "What in the world happened to you?" Emma didn't know what else to say, even though she already knew the answer. She had done this to him. She had done this to his spirit in the supernatural realm, and his body bore the scars.

"Don't be coy with me." His voice seeped forth in an uncertain rasp. "I have no patience for such tomfoolery today." He glanced at her arm. "At least you didn't come out of it unscathed."

That's when Captain Hernandez strode in. Two police officers followed.

Shaking, a bewildered Pompous Jack rose to face Hernandez. "What is the meaning of this?" His words lacked their normal confidence. Instead, they projected uncertainty.

Before the shocked man knew what was happening, the officers had circled the desk and snapped handcuffs on his wrists.

"Barney Clark, you are under arrest for—"

"You have no proof!" Pompous Jack's face tightened. He tried to move his arms, but the restraints corralled them.

"We have several years of security footage." The hint of a pleased smile played on Captain Hernandez's normally indifferent lips.

"Impossible! The files are overwritten every twenty-four hours."

"Not before they're uploaded to the cloud. We have a record of all the late-night guests who visited you at the Temple Palace. With facial recognition software, we've identified every one. They're not happy with you. They want to see you pay."

"Though some may disapprove of my proclivities," Pompous Jack sputtered, "there's nothing illegal about me entertaining attractive ladies at the palace."

"Four of them were minors. They've agreed to testify."

"It will never stick. I have powerful friends. They'll ruin you!"

"No, you've ruined yourself." The captain turned his attention to his agents. "Take him away."

As they dragged the flustered man from the room, he turned toward Emma. Desperation covered his face. "Do something, High Priestess," he croaked. "Save me."

"Not a chance."

"You know I've always had your best interest in mind. Stop this madness before it's too late."

"Approach the Sovereign with a pure heart and live," Emma quoted from her favorite passage. "Those with selfish intent will perish."

With a shudder, Pompous Jack recoiled at hearing those words from the Holy Text.

"You're getting exactly what you deserve," Emma said. "You'll go away for a long time, maybe the rest of your life. Then you won't be able to hurt anyone else."

"You think this is the end, Emma Barlow, but

it's not!" His shaky voice rose. "It's only the beginning."

If you enjoyed *Dueling the Devil,* please leave a review online. Your review will help others learn about this book and encourage them to read it too.

Thank you

REFORMING THE RELIGION

BOOK 4 OF THE NEXT HIGH PRIEST SERIES

Chapter 1: A New Day

Emma snickered. She giggled. Then she laughed. *Barney Clark.* Who would have thought the real name of her nemesis—in both this world and the spiritual realm—was Barney Clark? No wonder he had made up a title for himself. No wonder he insisted everyone call him His Royal Eminence.

Yet Emma never did. She had her own name for him: Pompous Jack. This nickname, however, wasn't out of disrespect as much as reflecting his character as a pompous jerk.

Yet with the arrest of Pompous Jack—that is, the arrest of Barney Clark—she was now safe. She could move forward, unopposed, in her new role as High Priestess.

Emma bowed her head. "Thank you, Sovereign, for protecting me and rescuing me from that evil man. Guide me in how to move forward to do your will here at the Temple. Amen."

She had a plan. With the Sovereign's guidance, she always had a plan. She pulled out her phone to review her list of projects:

- Divide priests into 3 groups
- Find out what's happening with Temple donations
- Improve working conditions for staff
- Restart Temple school
- Change rules so Topher and Ashley can date
- Help Topher's bedridden dad
- Find teaching job for Jennifer
- Find better role for Junior

Yes, it was ambitious, but she could already check off two items: dividing the priests into groups and a teaching job for Jennifer. Then she added a new item to the bottom of the list: *Help priests grow in their faith, be less lazy, not as demanding.*

Next, she inserted three sub-points under *Improve working conditions for staff.*

1. More pay
2. Less work
3. Increased respect

These additions matched the three points of the workers' protest, which she had joined, until the guard attacked her and the evil Barney Clark confined her to quarters.

These weren't greedy requests from the workers. All three points were legitimate. From what Emma had determined, each Temple employee earned minimum wage and never got a day off. Pompous Jack—Barney Clark—had also compelled them to donate their overtime hours. He didn't respect them, he didn't pay them enough, and he certainly overworked them. She needed to fix that. But first she had to find the money to do it. That was the second item on her list.

She added one more line, as prompted by the Sovereign: *Reopen health clinic for staff.* This was a desperate need because Barney Clark had made sure the Temple was exempt from providing healthcare insurance, even though it was the law for everyone else.

Then Emma entered what she hoped would be a final item: *Free the prisoners.*

Emma scanned all that she had to do. Even though she had checked off two items, she had added six more lines. Her to-do list was getting longer, not shorter. The enormity of the tasks in front of her filled her with dread. It overwhelmed her. And she had to work all these things around school.

Yet, she remembered that the Sovereign often said, "Trust me."

Emma intended to do just that.

In a hurry, she showered and dressed for the day. She scurried from her quarters in the Temple Palace and headed down the hill to the cafeteria. Walking in the morning's cool filled her with joy: inhaling fresh air, spending time outside, and getting her blood pumping. Though she would miss her private time with Jennifer at each meal, she was relieved to no longer have someone waiting on her like she was someone special. It just felt wrong.

As she neared the cafeteria, Junior exited the lower level of the priest compound and walked up to her. Emma had felt an instant connection with him when they first met a couple of days ago. She already had great respect for him, and she'd need his guidance as she sought to reform religious practices at the Temple.

"I thought I'd join you for breakfast." Junior matched her stride. Though Emma wasn't tall for her age, she was above average. Junior stood only a couple of inches taller. Yet while she was lean, he wasn't. Portly might be a polite description. Junior was a portly priest, yet a most endearing one. He seemed like a huggable teddy bear.

"Great!" Emma smiled. Aside from his company at breakfast, it would also mean less work for the Temple staff. "What did your server say when you told her?"

"She was surprised at first and then thanked me."

"And now she's got less work to do." Though this small step wouldn't allow Emma to cross another line off her list, she was at least moving in that direction.

"Not really." Junior's directness deflated Emma's short-lived optimism. Then he clarified. "She was assigned to deliver food for five priests. Now she has four. Any improvement is incremental at best."

This truth dampened Emma's enthusiasm. But

an idea formed in her mind as they ate breakfast. "Junior, will you schedule a meeting with the priests in Gamma group this afternoon? Let's do 1:30."

He dipped his head is if to start a nod but then glanced at Jennifer, who had joined them for breakfast. "What about your schooling?"

"Not a problem." Jennifer spoke with confidence. "Emma's smart and focused. We can easily finish her schoolwork before noon every day. That leaves afternoons open for her to attend to matters here at the Temple."

"Consider it done." Junior pulled out his phone and typed a quick message. "I have the Gamma priests set up for a group text chat."

"Let's do Beta group on Friday and Alpha group next Monday. Same time, same place."

"I'll make it happen."

Emma then added one more request. "If you have time while I'm in school, could you try to figure out what Barney's been up to?"

"A most excellent suggestion. I'll start with the office he's been using in the Temple Palace."

Emma turned her attention to Jennifer. "What if we add two people to our homeschool?" Her pitch increased as she made her request, peaking with the last word, which whimpered out as a wispy question. She scolded herself for coming across as weak, unsure. She'd need to work on her delivery if people were to respect her as High Priestess.

Emma tried again. "What if we add two people to our homeschool?" This time she lowered her tone and said *homeschool* with confidence and not an airy hesitance.

As if aware of what Emma had done, Jennifer dipped her head in approval. "Are you thinking of Chloe? And Joshua?"

"Yes! Joshua's mom was going to start home-schooling him next week, but she's already super busy. And Chloe's dad is checking into distance learning for her. We could help with both if you could homeschool them too."

"That would mean extra work for me." Jennifer scrunched up her face but then recovered. "I'm up to the challenge!"

"Except for biology," Emma said, "we have the same classes. I take honors bio, and they take regular bio. So it shouldn't be too much more work for you."

"Just be aware that our focus is on education and not spending time with your best friend or pursuing romance."

"Got it!" Then Emma considered more fully

what Jennifer had said. She would need to be sure to keep her education a priority. They all would. "I see your point, but we could help each other learn and study. So I think it's a good thing."

"I don't see adding them as a problem." Jennifer spoke as if processing her thoughts aloud. "They'll need to fill out the same paperwork as you did." Then she grew somber. "But let's not add any more to our roster, or I'll effectively be running a small school instead. That requires a lot more paperwork, more hoops to jump through . . . and more work for me."

"I'll text them as soon as school is over."

"Why not text them now?" Jennifer said. "We have thirty minutes before school starts."

Emma pulled out her phone, but a message from Captain Hernandez caught her attention. She gasped over what she read. "Be advised that Barney Clark has posted bond and will soon be released."

Continue this story in *Reforming the Religion*, Book 4 of The Next High Priest Series.

ABOUT PETER DEHAAN

Peter DeHaan is an adult who dreams of being a teenager. When he's not contemplating grown-up thoughts, his mind retreats to the domain of invented worlds with his loyal and most real, yet still imaginary, friends. What grand adventures they have: righting wrongs, solving problems, and making their world a better place to live.

His first published adventures come to life in "The Next High Priest Series"—a faith-friendly speculative fiction adventure in a world just like ours . . . only different.

Next up is *The Curious Gift*, a YA contemporary novella with a hint of the supernatural.

Then comes "The Ice Creamed Series," a present-day quest for friendship and love, all the while trying to survive high school unscathed and ping-ponging between responsible impulses and irresponsible slipups.

Want more? Get a free short-story prequel about Emma along with news of upcoming books when you sign up to receive Peter's updates at PeterDeHaan.com/fiction.

FICTION BOOKS BY PETER DEHAAN

The Next High Priest Series

Seeking the Sovereign

Confronting the Chaos

Dueling the Devil

Reforming the Religion

Freeing the Prisoners

Fighting the Fanatics

Perfecting the Priesthood

Pursuing the Politicians

Restoring the Repentant

Get a free short-story prequel about Emma along with updates of upcoming books when you sign up for Peter's fiction newsletter at PeterDeHaan.com/fiction.